Summer RAIN

CHERLISA STARKS RICHARDSON

Cherlisa Starks Richardson

INDIANAPOLIS

Purple Phoenix Publishing LLC
Indianapolis, IN

This book is a work of fiction. Any references to historical events, real people, or real places are used fictitiously. Other names, characters, places, and events are products of the author's imagination, and any resemblance to actual events or places or persons, living or dead, is entirely coincidental.

Copyright © 2013 by Cherlisa Starks Richardson

All rights reserved, including the right to reproduce this book or portions thereof in any form whatsoever.

Purple Phoenix Publishing LLC trade paperback edition December 2013.
Request wholesale book orders at www.cherlisarichardson.com.

ISBN 978-0-9910950-0-1

Cover Design by: Gabrielle Prendergast
Interior Layout by: A Reader's Perspective
Editing by: EBM Professional Services

Printed in the United States of America

For Clarence, Cayla, and Mama

*In memory of
Charles R. Starks, Sr. and Robert G. Douglas
(I was blessed to have two amazing fathers in my life)*

Acknowledgements

First, thank you, Lord, for allowing my dream of finishing this book to become a reality. Thanks for planting a seed and watering it as you guided my pen to tell the story you wanted me to tell. To God be the glory!

Next, I thank my family for their undying support. A special thanks to my husband, Clarence, for supporting me and hanging in there throughout this long process. To my daughter, Cayla, thank you for believing in me and for your patience throughout this process. I hope seeing this end product is yet another reminder that if you can dream it, you can achieve. This is for you, Love Bug. To my mother, Elizabeth, thank you for always believing in me and encouraging me. Thank you for instilling greatness in me and for teaching me that there isn't anything I can't do if I put my mind to it. To my sister, Dorothy and my cousin, Marie "Ree-Ree", thank you for sharing your medical knowledge and terminology with me. To my brother, Charles, Jr. and my Goddaughter, Bria (and Cayla too) thank you for your help with different lingo. ☺

A special thanks to my friends. To my BFF, Amanda McCoy-Collins, thank you. You were there as always supporting

100 percent from the beginning when this book was just an idea. To Gordon Meredith, thank you for your support and encouragement. To my girl, Sherry Harris, thanks for your unwavering support. To Stacy Hanks and Larry Adkins, thank you for sharing your knowledge as police officers.

A special thanks to my literary friends. To my diva friends, my sister girls, Daphine Glenn-Robinson (Author of *Too Many Lies*) and Donna Deloney (Author of *A Decent Proposal*), thank you, thank you, thank you for everything. You all have been there for every single step in this process. Thanks for always having my back. To my girl, my little big sister, Nakia Laushaul (Author of *Chasity Rules*), thank you for your encouragement and for pushing me to just do it. No more tags. ☺ To Rhonda McKnight (Author of *Breaking All the Rules*), thank you for being a great mentor and friend. To Daryl Green (Author of *Writing for Professionals*), thank you for your encouragement from day one. To Sandra LaVenchi (Author of *When the Grass Wasn't Greener on the Other Side*), thanks for being there. Our brainstorming sessions are always a blast. To Kimberla Lawson Roby (Author of *The Prodigal Son*), thank you for your support and kindness. Finally, I don't want to leave out my newest author friends. Berta Coleman (Author of *Honor My Father…Really?*), thanks for your encouragement and for being so sweet. To my homegirls, Stacy Campbell (Author of *Dream Girl Awakened)* and Tracy Cooper (Author of *Fannin' Old Flamez)* Tracy, Isn't it funny that we've actually known each other since college? ☺, the three of us connecting the way we did was no coincidence. I'm so excited for the great things ahead. The sky is the limit!

To my high school journalism teacher, Olivia Gonzales, who went home to be with the Lord on September 22, 2013, thank you for your love, support, and for nurturing my love for writing all those years ago when I was the editor of the Crispus Attucks high school yearbook. I love you and miss you. You'll live in my heart forever.

To my awesome editor, Michelle Chester, EBM Professional Services, thank you! It was a pleasure working with you. To my amazing typesetting, Nakia Laushaul, A Reader's Perspective, I appreciate you so much. Thank you. To Ira Mallory, BJYL Productions, thank you for bringing my book to life in the form of a book trailer. Your work is impeccable.

To my readers, thank you for supporting all my work so far—blog posts, articles, and social media postings. Thank you for continuing this journey and for your continued support by purchasing this book. Of all the books that are out there that you could have purchased, you chose *Summer Rain*. I appreciate that and I appreciate you. I hope you enjoy reading about Summer's journey and I pray it inspires you.

To everyone that ever said an encouraging word or supported me in any way, thank you! You know who you are and I appreciate you.

Peace and Love,

Cherlisa

Summer RAIN

CHAPTER 1

Summer

SUMMER BROWSED THROUGH the different messages posted on Facebook. Nothing new, just the same old stuff teens usually post—pictures of girls with duck lips posing in the latest fashions, boys and girls posing in the mirror holding up their phones, and corny jokes. Sometimes an occasional shot is made at some unsuspecting kid. *OMG! Am I reading this right?* Summer lifted her head from the headboard of her bed and pulled her iPad closer to her face. Her eyes grew wider as she stared at the screen. Maybe her eyes were playing tricks on her. She hadn't been getting much sleep lately. She blinked to see clearer. The kids at East High had gone completely crazy. Hadn't their parents preached the same message to them that hers drilled into her about watching what you post on the Internet? They had no shame in their game and didn't care who got hurt when they went in on people. The ruthless words they were calling Megan on her page were enough to make even the loosest girl want to crawl under a rock.

Summer read the last comment then turned off her iPad. She'd only gotten on the Internet as a distraction to help keep her awake. She had no idea what she was getting into when she logged onto Facebook. As soon as she thought the kids at her school couldn't get any meaner, they were taking it to a new level. She couldn't forget the worst comment about Megan—*I hope you die. You're too nasty to live.* Summer's mouth fell open when she read it. *How could anyone be that mean? Then again, why am I surprised?* That was the norm at East High. Every other week there was a new target.

Granted, everyone agreed that Megan brought the name calling on herself to some extent. Rumor had it she was trying to get the attention of one of the jocks on the basketball team. Everyone was saying that when she couldn't get his attention by flirting with him, she went so far as to join the cheerleading squad. That didn't work, so she resorted to sending him nasty text messages. When he didn't respond to that, she eventually made the dumb mistake of sending him the picture that made her infamous. She was posing on a bed with nothing on but her bra and panties. *Who does that?* That's when everything hit the fan. The boy posted the picture on Instagram using an anonymous account. All of the kids that followed him on the account sent it to their friends who sent it to their friends until it had made its way around the entire school. The hallways were buzzing with the same question every day—who started the picture going around? Whoever the dude was, he was keeping his identity a secret.

The strange thing was no one even knew who Megan was before the picture scandal. But that had all changed, and fast. From that point on, she couldn't walk down the hall without being called out of her name or being pushed and shoved around. She had officially become popular, for all the wrong reasons. Her reputation was in the toilet and there seemed to be no turning back.

Her locker was covered in graffiti. All types of dirty words covered it. Any normal person would think the administrators of the school would have had it removed immediately. It took them over a week to have it painted over, only for the graffiti to return the next day.

Summer sat her iPad on her nightstand. She turned on her iPod and skipped through several songs until she got to one of her favorite ones. She laid back on her pillow hoping the music would help her to forget about how bad Megan must feel.

"Summer?"

Summer's body froze at the sound of her mother's voice. *Dang.* She must have had the volume too high. She lay stiff in her bed with her eyes closed. She hoped her mother would believe she was sound asleep. She wasn't about to let her know that she had been awake since she lay down hours ago at 10:00 p.m.

"Summer, are you still up?" her mom, Simone, called again, turning on the light. Standing in the doorway with her hand firmly planted on her petite hip and her hair pulled back in a ponytail, Simone frowned as she waited for a response.

"Yes, Mom?" Summer replied, faking grogginess and rubbing her eyes while sitting up.

Simone's demeanor softened. "Oh, I'm sorry, honey. I didn't mean to wake you. I figured you had to be awake with that music playing so loud."

"It's okay. I guess I fell asleep listening to it. I didn't realize it was so loud." She turned down the volume.

"I hope you can go back to sleep. Have a good night, honey."

"I will. Good night." Simone turned off her light and closed the door behind her as she left the room.

Summer waited to hear her mom's footsteps down the hall and took a deep breath. She closed her eyes and lay back on her pillow. She shivered, rubbing the goose bumps on her arms. She didn't know if the chill that swept over her was from the cool air blowing from the window she'd opened earlier in a desperate attempt to stay awake, or from the fear of almost being caught by her mother. How long could she go on with this charade of pretending to sleep at night? Simone McClain was a teacher who had many years of training reading kids, and she was nobody's fool. It was only a matter of time. Summer wished she could get some rest but sleeping terrified her. *Why do I keep having that crazy nightmare?* It haunted her night after night, and she couldn't make any sense of it.

Her eyes felt heavy. The sound of one of her favorite R&B artist made her relax. *I have to stay awake.* She skipped through the next couple of songs in her playlist searching for something more upbeat. *I hope this works.* She turned on her side and faced the window. She watched the back and forth rhythm of her pink and white flowered curtains swaying with the rhythm of the wind. Her eyes began to close. She batted them to stay awake. Not even the fresh air was helping anymore. She tossed and turned and hummed to the music, trying to distract herself from the sleepiness that was overtaking her. None of it worked. She lost the fight. Her mind drifted to the place she'd tried so hard to keep it from going.

I walked down the streets of downtown Chicago with my parents, David and Simone McClain and my grandmother, daddy's mother, who everyone called Big Momma. The sweltering sun beamed down on us as we carried our lawn chairs and water coolers. Beads of sweat bounced off my golden bronze forehead. My black tresses no longer bounced with curls but lay limp on my shoulders. It had to be the hottest summer we'd had in a long time.

The closer my family got to Michigan Avenue, the more we anticipated the Fourth of July fireworks, and the more festive the atmosphere felt. My nose filled with the savory scents of barbequed food as we walked past clusters of people grilling hotdogs, hamburgers, chicken, and ribs. Other people were camped out lying in the grass on blankets all throughout the park.

"Where in the world are we going to sit?" My mom perused the park for a space to squeeze into.

"It's crazy out here. We'll find somewhere," Daddy said.

While looking for a place to sit, we ran into my best friend, Jasmine, and her mom, Victoria. After exchanging hellos our two families continued our search together for a place to hang out.

Thirty minutes passed and we were finally settled in near the lake, watching the sunset. The adults talked and laughed while Jasmine and I sat on a blanket playing cards. We laughed at the little girl riding the back of a Great Dane that was noticeably irritated but couldn't get away from the determined child's grip. Then there was the tattooed covered man that stood in the middle of the park, doing the moonwalk, listening to the radio in his head and singing his rendition of every Michael Jackson song that seemed to come to his mind.

A few hours later, we were all standing around in the dark, still talking and laughing when all of a sudden fireworks exploded in the sky one by one. Everyone's attention turned to the sky as it lit up with a rainbow of beautiful colors—red, white, blue, pink, green, and yellow. The reflection of the fireworks cast off the water of Lake Michigan. I smiled in awe. Although I'd gone to the show every year for as long as I could remember, it never lost its splendor in my eyes. We all stood looking up into the sky in amazement, our faces glowing from the light of the fireworks.

"*Daddy, look at that one! It's shaped like a heart with a bow and arrow.*" *Daddy smiled and looked down at me and wrapped his arm around my shoulders. A loud explosion sounded and the fireworks continued filling the sky as we all looked on.*

"*Get outta the way!*"

"*Aaaaaaaahhh!*"

A large woman dragging a boy behind her bumped into me and knocked my purse to the ground. What is her problem? I turned around to see why the woman was being so rude, only to see that several other people were running toward us as well. A tall man knocked over one of our lawn chairs and hurdled over our water cooler to keep from falling down. My eyes grew wide, a knot forming in the pit of my stomach. I turned to my father, desperately looking for direction. He was looking around with the evidence of concern on his face.

"*Stay calm. I have to see what's going on.*" *Daddy was a veteran police officer. I knew he was trying to come up with a plan. He was trained to think fast.*

"*He's got a gun!*" *someone yelled.*

"*Daddy, no!*" The knot in my stomach grew tighter.

"*Those are gunshots. Let's go! We need to get outta here. Now!*" Daddy yelled.

The sound of gunshots rang repeatedly in the air. Everyone was running and pushing to get away.

"*Go! That way!*" Daddy shouted, pointing in the direction everyone else was running.

"*What about Big Momma? And Mom?*"

"*Go baby! I'm okay. I'm right with you.*" My mom cried.

"*I've got Big Momma. You all go!*" My father said.

Big Momma was trying as hard as she could to get away. Seeing her struggle broke my heart but I did as I was told. I joined my mom, Jasmine, and Ms. Victoria, running alongside the other people that were frantically trying to distance themselves from the gunshots. I had almost reached Michigan Avenue when I turned around to see if my family was still with me. Everyone was behind me except for my father. I could hear him yelling, "*Go!*" but I couldn't see him. Several people had been trampled to the ground.

"*Daddy! Where are you? Are you okay?*" My lungs filled with air. I tried to speak again, but nothing came out.

"*Daddy,*" was all I could manage. My voice was drowned out by the screams of children and adults mixed with the gunshots. The gunshots. The sound was piercing my ears. I stood in the middle of the chaos, covering my ears.

"*Daddy!*" He was nowhere in sight.

The people were closing in on me. I wanted my daddy to save me, but he wasn't there. Just his voice calling, "*Summer. Go! Don't stop.*"

The people kept coming toward me. I couldn't get away. I closed my eyes and covered my head to protect myself. I screamed.

With a sudden jolt, Summer sat straight up. She looked around. Even in the dark, the neon pink walls were familiar. She then looked down at her pink and green flowered comforter. It was barely hanging on her bed, as the sheets tangled around her legs. She pulled the soft comforter up to her chest and nestled it under her chin. She took a deep breath and whispered, "Thank God."

Although cool air filled the room, her pajamas were stuck to her clammy, sweat-drenched body. The loose, long, black curls she usually wore were limp, stuck to her face. She wiped the sweat from her forehead with the back of her hand.

There was a knock on the door. David poked his head in her room. "Are you okay, sweetie?"

"Yes, Daddy. I just… I saw a spider."

"You should be sleeping, honey. Look what time it is. It's 2:30 in the morning."

"I know. I just had to go to the bathroom. That's why I was awake. Then when I lay back down, that's when I saw the spider."

"You sure it was just a spider?" He frowned.

"Yes, sir. I'm fine now. Thanks, Daddy." That was a hint for him to leave.

"Ummm hmmm. Good night. Or should I say, good morning?" David looked at Summer doubtfully. "I'm not so sure about that spider story but we'll let it go." Summer faked a smile. David blew her a kiss.

"I love you, pumpkin." He closed the door.

Summer leaned back on her headboard. The same nightmare had been haunting her for over a month. Big Momma always said, "Dreams have a meaning. God talks to us through our dreams." But what did hers mean? Why was she dreaming of great times she'd had with her family and friend, only to have it turn into what seemed like a live horror movie? It just didn't make sense. What she did know was that being up every night with these nightmares had caused her to be really tired. She wanted them to go away. Forever.

Her parents promised her they would take her to get help if the nightmares continued. *How is a doctor going to help me stop having nightmares? I don't want to go to a shrink.* Summer began to pray. *God, please, please make the horrible nightmares go away. I'm exhausted. I'm terrified to go to sleep. If You would just make them go away I'll do all the right things. I promise God. Well, except for one little thing and I hope You forgive me for this. I know it's wrong to keep things from my parents but I've decided, I really need to keep these nightmares that I'm still having between me and You. Will You forgive me? Amen.* Afraid to close her eyes again, she reached in her nightstand drawer and pulled out a small energy drink bottle. It would hold her over for at least five hours, and then she would take another one to get her through the next day at school. That evening she'd be hanging out with Jasmine and Antoine at the boys varsity basketball game. No doubt that would be enough excitement to keep her wide awake. With all the Facebook drama, all eyes would definitely be on Megan who would be cheering on the sideline. She turned up the bottle of liquid energy until it was empty. She laid her head on her pillow and stared at the ceiling until her alarm went off a few hours later.

CHAPTER 2

Summer

"That game was goooood! I still can't believe Brandon made five three-point shots in one quarter. And did you see those dunks Dre made?" Summer said.

"Who didn't? I thought I was watching an NBA team. It was definitely the best game of the season." Jasmine agreed. She took her book out of her locker. "But the real drama was with Megan."

"Yeah that was real crazy! Those girls are crazy. I felt so bad for her the way they were ignoring her like she wasn't cheering right next to them. And then, that sign they had on her back saying, *I'm loose. Try me.* How did they put it on there without her knowing it?"

"Girl, Monique. She's so mean and manipulative. I wouldn't put anything past her. She's capable of anything. If it's mean, she can pull it off. And her little followers, Raquel and Macy, are always right there behind her like little puppies laughing at whatever she does."

"Well, everyone was laughing at Megan last night. I felt horrible for her. They are cra—" A shrill scream came from the ladies restroom a few feet from where they were standing.

A girl stumbled backwards out of the restroom, holding her hand to her mouth. Her hand did nothing to muffle the screaming or to control the panicked condition she was in. Summer and Jasmine rushed to the restroom along with everyone else to see what had her so upset. When they walked in, Summer stopped dead in her tracks. Megan's body hung lifelessly from the ceiling. Her head hung sideways from the noose that was around her neck. Her long blonde locks were draped over her face. Summer could feel her heart pounding. She turned towards the sink. There was a message on the mirror written in red lipstick: *Now I'm gone. I hope you're happy.* Tears rushed to Summer's eyes. Megan gave up. She couldn't take it anymore.

CHAPTER 3

David

DAVID MCCLAIN TOOK a sip of his coffee hoping it would give him the pick me up he needed. He couldn't believe it was Monday already. He looked at the stack of papers sitting on his desk and thought about the reports that were due by Wednesday. His head dropped on the stack of papers. *It is definitely Monday,* he thought. He sat up, then took another sip of coffee.

Eighteen months ago he was asked to leave his job as a patrolman and lead the departments Student Advocacy program, a program where designated police officers are assigned to the public schools with the purpose of mentoring students to help improve crime rates, reduce the dropout rate, improve grades, and be available during crisis situations. David knew it wouldn't be an easy job but he was up for the challenge. Crime in the schools was getting worse and the department needed to do something fast. David's boss was confident he was the answer to their problem.

David looked across the room at Jay Lopez, his best friend

and partner, who sat at his desk with a grimace on his face. He knew the reason for Jay's frustration was also paperwork. Fortunately, there were times when backup was needed or when there was no one else available for a run, then David and Jay would take the call. It didn't look like that was going to happen today. They'd been in the office a few hours and their phones hadn't rung and all the radio calls seemed to be getting picked up. David took a deep breath and reached in the stack and grabbed a folder.

Jay took one file at a time spreading them across his desk as if he couldn't decide where he wanted to begin. "You know, I still think it's messed up how I got thrown into this job because you're always acting like Officer Friendly."

"Yeah, you tell me at least once a week." David continued writing and didn't look up.

"They act like we're inseparable. I would have been just fine staying on the streets as a patrolman."

David looked up. "You know good and doggone well you didn't want another partner. And who else would put up with you anyway?" He laughed.

"You got jokes. I didn't sign up for all this."

"I got jokes but you're always calling me Officer Friendly. Okay." David smiled and shook his head.

David was almost done with a report about a kid who was caught with drugs in his locker when the telephone rang.

"Officer McClain." He listened intently to the person on the other end of the phone. His face became troubled. "Do you have a name?" David paused, and then let out a sigh of relief.

"Okay, we'll be right over." He dropped the phone on its base and reached for his coffee cup as he stood.

"That was Sergeant Anderson. We need to head over to Summer's school. A girl's body was found hanging in the bathroom." David's first instinct was to make sure Summer was okay. Other than a name, Sergeant Anderson hadn't given any details on the circumstances surrounding the death, but either way, it wasn't good. A girl was dead. Not only did he have to help deal with that but he knew he had to remain low key about the fact that he was Summer's father, as he always did when he went to her school. When he took the position, they'd decided that was best for them both.

Jay dropped the file on his desk. "Another day in the life. Let's do it."

Hours later, David was relieved to be home. He knew he had to talk to Summer. He wouldn't rest until he made sure of a few things. She was laying on the couch when he walked in the house.

"Daddy, did you hear about what happened at my school today?" Summer sat up as he entered. Her voice quivered; her eyes were red and teary.

"Yes, honey. I've been there most of the day with the investigators." He dropped down on the couch next to her, took a deep breath, and put his arm around her shoulder. Their paths didn't cross because the school was on lockdown and the students were held in the gymnasium away from the bathroom that had become a crime scene.

"I can't believe Megan killed herself."

"How well did you know her?"

"I didn't know her at all until about a month ago."

"Do you know of a reason why she would have wanted to kill herself?"

Summer frowned and looked away from her father.

"Well?"

She sat up a little straighter. "Well, no one really knew her until… until a picture of her wearing only her underwear went around the whole school."

David frowned. Summer went through the whole series of events explaining everything to him that happened to Megan, beginning with her liking the boy all the way up to the basketball game when she ran out crying.

David felt like someone stabbed him in his heart. He couldn't stop thinking how that could have been his daughter. It was times like these he felt he failed at his job. What else could he have implemented in the schools that could have prevented this? He was supposed to be able to stop these types of things from happening. "Honey, you know you can talk to your mom and me about anything, right?"

Summer looked confused. "Sure, Daddy. Why are you asking that?"

"My heart breaks for her parents. I'd bet Megan never talked to them about what was going on with her. I'd bet money on it, especially since that picture of her was involved. I just want you to know that no matter how bad a situation ever gets, you can talk to us about anything."

"Yes, you and Mom have told me that for as long as I can remember." She was right. They had told her that many times before but he wanted to make sure. The thought of losing her over some nonsense nearly brought him to tears.

"You're sure?"

"Yes, Daddy, I know." She smiled then reached over and hugged him. She could obviously tell he was worried. "I would talk to you and Mom. Really, I would, but I wouldn't even let those stupid kids get to me like that. I definitely wouldn't let them push me to kill myself."

David was glad to see Summer's confidence was still intact.

"The other thing I want you to understand. And I really want you to get this. Okay?"

"O-kayyy?"

"Please understand that in life you're going to have problems. When it seems like you won't get through them, you will. You have to go on because God has a purpose for each one of our lives. Throwing in the towel and giving up is not an option. People do that far too often. Especially young people. There are an increasing number of teen deaths every year due to suicide, because when young people go through things, many times it's the first challenge they've had in their life. They can't imagine it will ever get better or don't see a way out. That's when they should seek help. That's why I do the work I do every day."

"I know I can talk to you and Mom. I'm okay, Daddy. I promise."

"Okay, honey." David let out a breath. He was satisfied for the time being.

CHAPTER 4

David

Two months had passed since Megan committed suicide. With school out for the summer, David's frustration grew because the detectives hadn't been able to pinpoint the students that had been bullying Megan or even the boy she had been pursuing. None of the kids would talk. David wanted the detectives to go beyond the basic interviews and go into the neighborhoods where they could catch the kids where they were most comfortable. Since he and Jay were doing more patrol work with school being out, he'd been doing a little investigation of his own. He hoped he'd get some answers real soon.

He stopped at the door before heading out to work for the day. He strapped and secured his gun belt around his waist. "I love you, babe." He leaned over and kissed Simone.

"I love you too, honey. You have a good day and stop stressing." Simone rubbed her finger across his lips and wiped off the remnants of lipstick she'd left behind.

"You know. As hard as I've been trying, I guess I haven't done a very good job of hiding my stress from you," David admitted.

"Uh, no. It's been seventeen years. I don't know why you still try. You always give it away when you put your head in your hands and rub your temples."

"Oh, yeah. I was doing that again, huh? Well, I want you not to worry about me and enjoy yourself today. This summer is halfway over and it's been no different than all the previous ones. While—"

"I know. I know."

"I know you know but I'm going to say it anyway. While other teachers have been relaxing and enjoying their time off, all you've been doing is things around the house, gardening, tutoring kids, and running around doing things for me, Summer, Big Momma, and your friends. Today is your day. So, don't you worry about me. I'll be just fine. You go and enjoy your day with the girls." He planted a kiss on her lips.

"I will. I will. And thank you again for treating me to a getaway." Simone smiled and winked.

"Don't detour from your plans today." He gave her a stern look followed by another kiss on the cheek before turning to walk out the door. Simone laughed.

Summer ran from her bedroom and caught him at the door. She embraced him with a big hug. "Bye, Daddy. I'll see you later. Love you!"

"I love you too, sweetie." Leaning down, he kissed her on her forehead. "Have a good day and make sure Mom does too."

"I will." She smiled looking at her mom.

"Alright, sweet pea. Daddy's got to go."

Summer frowned, crossing her arms.

"What?" David asked with a mischievous smile, trying to pretend he didn't know what she was going to say.

"Daddy, really? I'm sixteen years old. Almost *seventeen*. And you're still calling me sweet pea like I'm a little girl."

"That's because you're still *my* little girl and you always will be, so don't forget it." David planted another kiss on her forehead. "Now have fun today."

"Bye, Daddy."

David looked at her bright smile as he walked off the porch and headed down the driveway. He was actually glad his little girl would get a chance to relax at the spa also. He'd noticed the past couple of months she'd been showing signs of exhaustion. She said she wasn't having the nightmares anymore but he wasn't so sure.

"Hi, Mr. McClain," yelled Jasmine from the car as she and her mother drove up in front of the house.

"Hi, Jasmine, Victoria. Jasmine, you girls have a good time today, okay?" David smiled.

"We're going to have a real good time. Bye, Mr. M. Bye, Mom."

"See you all later." He waved as he drove off.

A couple of hours later, David checked in at the station, then he and Jay hit the streets. They were enjoying their summer schedule being back on patrol. Their first stop of the day, as usual, was Starbucks for their regular cup of Joe and a glazed donut. As they walked toward the door, the aroma of fresh-brewed coffee filled his nose. David took a deep breath.

They walked in and the barista already had two large cups of coffee and two pastries individually packaged and ready for them. They paid the cheerful cashier and dropped a few dollars each in the tip jar.

"Bye, Officers. I'll see you guys tomorrow. Have a good day." The barista handed Jay his cup accompanied by a flirty smile. Jay seemed to have that effect on women where ever they went.

"You too." David chuckled, shaking his head.

Jay grinned. "See you tomorrow."

They began their patrol, engaging in their usual topics of conversation, mainly Jay's relationship with his longtime girlfriend, Zoe.

"So how are things with Zoe?"

"Man, same stuff, different day."

"Dude, you and Zoe have been together forever. She's a beautiful woman. What's really going on with you?"

"You already know. We've been through this too many times before."

"And I keep telling you, marriage is a good thing." David laughed, looking ahead as he drove.

"Man, you're laughing but I'm serious. As great as I know Simone is and as much as I've come to love her like she's my own sister," he let out a laugh, "I don't know how you do it. You give up all of your freedom. You can't hang out with your boys anymore because your wife is there constantly nagging you and telling you what to do, when to do it, and exactly how it should be done. You're not an individual anymore."

David tried to compose his laughter enough to speak. "Jay man, are you serious? I've told you before, it's not like that. True, you do have to make some changes in your life because you have to consider that your life now includes someone else. But that doesn't mean that you have to lie down and die, man. It's just a compromise. If you're with someone who loves you and you love them, you really want it to work." He paused, thinking about how much he loved Simone. "You find a way to make it work. You realize that giving up a few things you did as a single man is really worth it in order to make things work with the person you love. You also realize that being with the woman you love and making her happy is worth way more than the things you gave up. Trust me, man. I'm a living witness."

"Yeah, that's what you say, but when it's all said and done, I know when you get home, the shackles are still on."

David almost choked, letting out a laugh. "Shackles? I'm telling you, it's not like that. Let me ask you a question. Does Zoe know how you feel about marriage?"

"No, not really. She hints around about it every once in a while, but I usually just tell her we're going to always be together and then change the subject. You know as well as I do if I tell her how I feel that would only stir up problems that I *don't* want to deal with."

"Okay, so you said she's hinted, which more than likely means she wants to get married. Then you said you told her that you two will be together forever, which means you're leading her to believe you *want* to be married. I know we've been laughing about your whole theory on marriage, but seriously, if she really wants to be married, wouldn't it be only right for you to let her know how you feel?"

"Dude—"

"I'm serious. Eventually she's going to bring it up and you're going to have to deal with the issue. Anyway, it's wrong to lead her on to believe you want to be married but have no intentions of going through with it. It's not right, and what's going to end up happening is you're going to lose her all together if you don't deal with that subject at some point."

Jay grimaced. "I hear you but I'm not opening that can of worms, and Zoe loves me. Trust me. She's not going anywhere."

David turned the corner. "Man, you know—" He stopped the car as he looked to his right. "Look over there."

"Man, look at those guys. You know they are up to something. I'm so sick of these losers." Jay was referring to a group of three young guys with sagging pants holding beer bottles and three skimpily dressed girls huddled together on a corner. A tall guy stood in the middle of another huddle while several other guys handed him money. Jay had worked on the streets for over ten years and he had no sympathy for drug dealers and gang bangers.

David made a U-turn and drove in their direction.

"You want me to call for back up?" Jay picked up the radio.

"Naw, we can handle this. By the time back up get here, they'll be scattered and whatever drugs they might have on them will be thrown away. Let's just see if we can talk some sense into them."

Jay shook his head. "You know it's a waste of time but if you insist."

David pulled the squad car up to the curb, making sure not to hit the beer bottle lying on the ground. The group that just moments earlier were deep into their activities and hanging out with ease was now acting very uptight and began to scuffle around, breaking away from their huddle. They began sticking their hands deep in their pockets and babbling to one another, attempting to walk away. The guy who had been taking money took off running down the street.

"Hey, stop right there," Jay yelled before anyone else could run.

"Hold up," a short guy said, holding his hand up toward his buddies, then turned to face the police officers who were now out of the car stepping on the trash as they walked toward them.

"How's everything going today, fellas?" David said.

"Wuz up?" said a taller, heavyset man. A couple of others tilted their chins up and back down as their way of saying hello. The others just looked at them.

"What's going on?" David inquired.

The shorter, bald guy responded, "Man, we just hangin' out. Mindin' our business."

"Man, look. Don't insult my intelligence. We know what's going on." Jay was becoming noticeably impatient with them.

"What do you mean you know what's going on? Do you see anything *going on?*"

"Look—" Annoyed, Jay raised his voice.

"Look guys," David interrupted. "Most of you look like you should be in school. You all need to clean up your act and make some serious choices for your lives. Right now, with what you're doing, you are headed in one of two directions. Do you know what that is?"

"Naw man, what's that?" The big guy looked around at the others, and they all laughed.

"I'm sure it does seem funny now, but to answer your question, jail or the grave. This is a life with a dead end."

They rolled their eyes and took a deep sigh. One guy threw his hands in the air and said, "Aw man."

One guy didn't have a reaction. David handed him a business card. "This is a local community center. Stop by and speak with a counselor. There are educational options and trades you can pick up. There are lots of things you could do that would be a better alternative." He took the card and stuck it in his pocket.

"I think the rest of you should check it out as well." He handed them each a card. "You guys stay out of trouble."

He and Jay walked back to their car. David watched them from the corner of his eye. He could see them throwing the cards on the ground. They all burst out into laughter.

"Man, that dude is crazy. What kind of money do he think somebody gon' make doin' that stuff he talkin' 'bout?" one of the guys blurted out, not caring that the police officers could still hear them.

"What a waste of time. You are really God sent because I don't have the patience that you do to deal with those guys like that. As a matter of fact, I don't know anyone that does," Jay said.

"Man, that's what I'm called to do. Make a difference in people's lives. So, I just do what I do. I realize what a lot of people don't."

"What's that?"

"Have you ever heard that hurt people hurt others?"

Jay frowned. "No I can't say that I have. So what are you getting at?"

"It's true. If you can get a person to see that they are hurting, they can begin to heal. When the healing process begins they'll realize that they've been hurting others. That's just the beginning. From there, if you can get them to see that they can be different, it's then that they can make a difference. You never know when maybe one will get what you're trying to tell them, like Antoine did."

"Yeah, but Antoine was just fourteen years old when we first met him and he was out here skipping school, hanging out on the streets with older guys. Although there are other guys out here the age Antoine was and younger, a lot of the people we run into are older than him. I don't know if there's really any hope for them."

"Antoine was younger than a lot of these guys and to be honest, that's what bothered me the most about him because he was the same age as Summer. He actually went to her school and had somehow gotten tied up with some drug dealers. He tried to play the tough guy role but I could still see the potential in him. Just like a lot of these guys out here. Even the older ones. That's why I kept talking to him and it's also why I don't give up on the rest of them. God can do anything. You remember. It took a lot to get through to Antoine. I mentored him for about a year before I was finally able to reach him. He got off the streets and began going to school. He was making good grades and stayed away from negative people. He turned his life around, man."

"Yeah, I hear you but you know those are really rare cases. There aren't many Antoine's out here."

"No one would have ever believed he would change. Like I said, God can do anything."

"Yeah, I guess," Jay responded. "Speaking of a waste of time, how did your last meeting go about finding the kids that bullied the girl who committed suicide?"

"Pretty much a dead end, so I've been doing a little research on my own."

"Right."

"I think I'm getting a little closer to narrowing it down. I think I have a pretty good idea who the guy is that started the picture going around. I just have to make sure first."

"That's good. Hey, since it's about time to head to lunch, go ahead and drop me off at my car and I'm going to head to my doctor's appointment."

"Cool."

As they were driving, the dispatcher's monotone voice came across the police radio. "Officer needed to take a report at The Towers." She rattled off an address. "Resident came home discovering that apartment had been burglarized. Caller gave no further information." A few minutes later the report was repeated.

"Great. I wonder why the guys in that area aren't responding," David said.

"Man you know they're probably sitting there ignoring the call and going on their way to lunch just like we're trying to do. I guess I'll cancel my appointment so we can head on over there."

"No, don't do that. It's only a report. I'll drop you off so you can make your appointment and I'll go on over there to take the report. I'm sure those guys are somewhere in the area. I'll meet up with them. It shouldn't take too long."

"Alright. If you insist."

"It's cool. It would be crazy for you to cancel your appointment."

Twenty minutes later after David took Jay to his car, he was headed toward The Towers. As he drove, he hoped it would be a quick run and he could be on his way to eat lunch. He was starving. In the back of his mind he just knew that whenever he wanted a simple report to go fast like it should be, it would take forever. His stomach was growling loud. He began thinking about what he could eat. *Do I want McDonald's or Burger King? Or maybe Subway?* His stomach growled louder. *Stop thinking about food, David.*

He drove in front of the apartment. "Great," he spoke out loud. None of the officers that normally covered that area were anywhere in sight. *I guess I'm the only one not at lunch right now.* Everything seemed pretty quiet in the area except for a few guys hanging out. The big groups of people drinking, gambling, and hanging all over the place weren't out there like they usually were.

He stepped out of his patrol car, walked up to the door of apartment 135, and knocked. As he stood at the door waiting for a response, the aroma of pork chops being deep fried on the other side of the door escaped and caused his stomach to growl again. *I wish they would hurry.* He knocked again and tried to wait patiently. After a few minutes a female voice yelled from the other side of the door.

"Who is it?"

"Chicago Police Department. I'm responding to a report of a burglary."

"How do I know you the po-leese? It could be another one of these fools around here pretending to be a cop, tryin' to take what they didn't get earlier. I see that uniform. Let me see yo ID if you really the po-leese."

Oh boy. Here we go. So much for a quick run. He took a deep breath and put his ID up to the peephole.

"Y'all show took y'all time coming and got the nerve to come right when I'm startin' my dinner. Hold on. I have to turn off the stove." The woman's voice faded but David could still hear her. "I'm not going to let my pork chops burn up cause y'all took y'all time. I'm sick of the po-leese and these fools around here." A few minutes later the door swung open and the boisterous woman stood in front of him with a red scarf on her head holding a dish towel. David was in utter shock.

"Are you gonna come in?"

With the invitation, David stepped inside the apartment trying not to step on the dirty clothes that covered the floor. The smell of pork chops was now fused with a stale, unclean scent. His hunger subsided.

The woman looked at David from head to toe. Her tone changed. "I'm cookin' dinner early. You hungry?"

David looked straight ahead into the kitchen and couldn't help but notice the dirty dishes that were piled high in the sink and on the table. The grayish color floor in the kitchen looked as if it hadn't been mopped in months. Suddenly, David felt sick to his stomach.

"No, thank you." He tried to force a smile. As he'd anticipated, this call would be anything but short. He didn't come out until an hour later.

CHAPTER 5

Simone

They'd finally made it to the spa, and the girls couldn't contain their excitement. Summer and Jasmine jumped out of the SUV, leaving Simone following behind them. She chuckled, shaking her head. She was glad they were looking forward to their spa day. David had certainly put a lot of planning into it.

When they opened the door to the spa, the smell of peppermint met their noses. Simone stopped for a moment and took a deep breath, taking in the sweet fragrance.

"Hello, ladies. My name is Lauren. Welcome to Tranquility Day Spa. Can I get you checked in?" the receptionist greeted.

"Hello, Lauren. We'll just wait for my friend to arrive and then we'll be ready."

"Your—"

"Hey, girl," someone said, cutting Lauren off.

Simone recognized the familiar voice behind her. A smile spread across her face as she turned around. It was Vivian, her best friend from college. She should have known. Early as usual. She hadn't seen her sitting on the couch behind her. Vivian stood and greeted Simone and the girls with a warm hug. Vivian's tall, slender frame lit up the room with her usual classy but casual style she always sported whenever she wasn't in the courtroom. She wore a designer white, sleeveless halter top that was gem studded at the top, jeans that looked like they were tailored just for her, black strappy sandals with a three inch heel, and two hundred dollar Dolce & Gabbana shades to match her large black leather satchel.

"I'm so happy to see you." Simone screeched. "I never see you with your crazy schedule, Ms. new corporate attorney for one of Chicago's largest law firms."

"Oh, stop. Although I have to admit, I am glad you made me promise to clear my calendar and not take any clients today. That's the only way you would get me away from the office. I thought I was busy before but I've been extremely swamped since becoming a partner. I needed this. Thanks, girl."

"Well, I'm glad you made it," Simone said, hugging her.

"Did I have a choice?" Vivian laughed.

"Well, you've got a point."

"Simone, you are looking so good and relaxed. How do you do it?"

"Girl, David had to make me take a day off for myself. So, believe me when I say, I may *look* relaxed but I *need* this day to be pampered. I didn't admit it to him but I'm exhausted." She threw her head back with her hand on her forehead and closed her eyes.

While the ladies were doing their hellos and chit-chatting, Lauren got them all checked in.

"Okay, ladies, you're all set. If you all are ready, Gina will take you back." Lauren pointed to the masseuse standing at the door.

"We're ready," Simone confirmed.

"If you ladies would follow me this way, we'll get you all started," Gina said.

They followed her as she led them to their very own private tranquility room. Immediately, Simone felt the tension begin to release from her body as her nose caught a whiff of the sweet scent of lavender that filled the dimly lit, purple room.

Summer's attention, however, was completely focused on the trays of delectable fresh strawberries, bananas, and pineapple chunks dipped in chocolate sitting on the table by each one of the sofas. She grabbed Jasmine by the arm and led her to one of the plush sofas and delved right into a juicy strawberry. The girls sat, nestled deep into the plush cushions eating the fruit. While they waited the next five minutes or so for their rooms to be prepared, Simone and Vivian caught up on all that had gone on since they last spoke.

Gina, the masseuse, interrupted, "Ladies, if you would follow me. It's time to prepare for your massages. Your masseuse's are ready. "

Everyone got up except for Summer, who had fallen asleep. Jasmine noticed Simone's concerned look, then reached out and placed a firm grip on Summer's arm and gave her an abrupt shake. "Wake up, Summer. It's time for our massage."

Startled, Summer opened her eyes and quickly perused the room. Her eyes stopped on Simone who was staring at her. "Oh, I'm awake. I guess I fell asleep for a moment." She stood and stretched. "Let's go." She wrapped her arm around her best friend and gave her a tight squeeze. She and Jasmine followed Vivian in the direction Gina had sent them.

Simone decided to spare her the interrogation, but she couldn't help being concerned. Why was Summer so exhausted? She said the nightmares had stopped, but now Simone wasn't so sure. Maybe David's suspicions were right, that Summer was still having the nightmares but was keeping it from them. Simone decided she wouldn't worry about it for the time being. She needed to relax. She made a mental note to pay closer attention to Summer's sleep pattern going forward, and then followed Vivian and the girls.

As Simone drove, she couldn't help but think what a great day it had been with her best friend and the girls. The full body massage was just what she'd needed. She felt relaxed in a way she hadn't in a long time. Gina had outdone herself earning an extra twenty dollars on top of her regular tip.

Summer and Jasmine sat in the backseat chattering and laughing. Simone smiled, glancing at them through her rearview mirror. Their rising voices didn't bother her at that moment. They knew she was a stickler about them not being too loud in the car in case of an emergency and she needed to hear a siren. For some reason, the more she drove a strange feeling of uneasiness came over her. A tight ball formed in the pit of her stomach. *What is going on with me? I hate this feeling. Shake it off, Simone. Today has been a good day. This is crazy.*

She continued driving and noticed that the clouds were getting very dark. *That must be it. It's going to rain and that's affecting me. This has been too good of a day for these clouds to destroy my mood.* She tried to shake it off by thinking of something different. "You know I couldn't convince Big Momma to come with us but I told her that I'd bring something home for dinner so she wouldn't have to cook. What do you think about pizza?"

"That works for me," Summer replied.

"Jazz, what about you? Are you staying for dinner?"

"Yes, ma'am. My mom just told me to call her when I was ready for her to pick me up."

"Great. I'll order as soon as we get in the house. I take it you all want the regular."

"Yes. Large, deep dish pepperoni."

"How did I guess?" Simone smiled. She hoped diverting her attention to the girls would help her forget the increasingly strange feeling that wouldn't leave the pit of her stomach. At least she was almost home. Maybe then she could sit down with David, Big Momma, and the girls and the feeling would go away.

She turned the corner onto her street. Flashing red and blue lights of police cars were down her street.

"I wonder what's going on." As she drove closer to her house, she realized the police were in her yard. *What's going on? Is something wrong with Big Momma?*

"Mom, the police are at our house. What could be wrong?" Summer's voice was shaky.

"Baby, I don't know but we'll find out in a few minutes. Just start praying."

"Okay." Summer's eyes welled up with tears.

Simone was struggling herself to hold back tears. The feeling in her stomach intensified as soon as she saw the flashing lights. She pulled into her driveway. Before she could get out, an officer was at her car opening the door for her.

"Mrs. McClain?"

"Yes?"

"Please, let me help you out of your car."

"It's okay. I'm fine." Simone stepped out of the car and stood directly in front of the officer. "What's going on?" She looked around and took notice of the other officers standing by their patrol cars. Then she noticed Big Momma standing next to one of the police cars talking to one of the officers.

He didn't answer her quick enough. "What is going on?" She was relieved to know that Big Momma was okay, but couldn't figure out what was going on.

"Why don't we go inside your house? It might be better to talk there."

"I don't want to go in the house. Tell me now. What's going on?"

"Ma'am, there's been an accident."

"What kind of accident? With who?" She thought she heard a pounding sound. It was her own heart racing.

"I'm sorry, ma'am. It's your husband, Officer McClain. He's been shot."

"No… No…" She fell to her knees on the driveway. She knew exactly what was wrong. Her worst nightmare had come true. She'd feared this for years.

"Mom!" Frantic, Summer ran from the other side of the car and stooped down next to her mom trying to console her.

"No… No… No…" Simone pounded her fist on the driveway. She didn't want to believe it. "Oh, no!" The tears were pouring from her eyes as blood dripped from her hand. "Is he… Is he…"

The officer responded quickly, "He's still alive, but he's in critical condition. We need to get you to the hospital right away."

"Okay." Simone looked around. Summer had heard the whole conversation and was now sobbing uncontrollably in Big Momma's arms. Big Momma had tears falling down her face but she stood strong trying to support Summer.

"It's going to be okay, baby. It's in God's hands," Big Momma said, rubbing Summer's arm.

Jasmine stood in the driveway and was ending a call on her cell phone.

"Mrs. M. I'm so sorry this has happened to Mr. M. My mom is on her way to get me. She said she's less than five minutes away and you shouldn't wait on her. She also said that she's sorry about what happened and she'll be lifting Mr. M. and the family in prayer."

"Tell her thanks for the prayers and we'll be in touch."

"Yes, ma'am." Jasmine went over and hugged her best friend and turned back toward the driveway to wait for her mom.

One of the female police officers insisted on caring for Simone's scraped up, bloody hand before they rushed her, Big Momma, and Summer into the police car.

"Thank you for the towel. I appreciate it. No need to clean my hand right now." Her hand throbbed but she couldn't think about herself. She needed to get to David. The loud sound of sirens roared, the red and blue lights flashed as they sped to Christ Memorial Hospital.

CHAPTER 6

Simone

THEY ARRIVED AT the hospital in what seemed to be five minutes flat. Simone tried to get as much information about what happened to David from the officer on their ride there, but to no avail. He would not offer her very much other than what she already knew. It occurred to her that he had already told her what he was authorized to tell. She understood his position. She'd been married to a cop for over seventeen years. She realized there were certain protocols to be followed, but at that moment, it heightened her anxiety. She needed to know that David would pull through this.

The officer pulled in front of the emergency doors and another officer opened the car door letting them out. They rushed through the hospital corridor. The stale smell that you only experienced in a hospital filled her nose but she hardly noticed it. Her mind was only on David. Her heart raced as her legs moved at lightning speed. Summer followed close behind her with Big Momma walking as fast as she could. Finally the police officer stopped at the nurse's station and spoke to the woman sitting behind the desk.

The woman picked up the phone. "Dr. Donaldson, please report to the nurse's station. Dr. Donaldson, please report to the nurse's station." She hung up the phone. "The doctor will be with you all shortly."

Simone nodded.

A few minutes later a doctor in blue scrubs came out and extended his hand toward Simone. "Hello, I'm Dr. Donaldson."

"Simone McClain," she said as she shook his hand.

"As you know, your husband, Officer McClain, was shot. He's in surgery right now and he's in critical condition. There's not a whole lot else I can tell you about his condition except we're doing everything we can to keep him—"

Simone gasped.

"Ma'am, I'm sorry. I don't want to alarm you but right now your husband isn't out of the woods. We'll be back out to update you once he's out of surgery."

"Thank you," Simone responded, feeling helpless.

Three hours later, Dr. Donaldson returned and told the family that David was out of surgery and they had him resting in a room. He escorted them to a room where there were two armed policeman standing on each side of the door.

The doctor nodded at the officers. The one to the right opened the door and stepped to the side for them to enter. Simone took a deep breath. She paused with her feet planted on the floor. She looked up and said a silent prayer for strength and then walked into the room. The tears that had finally slowed down during the ride to the hospital had returned in full force.

She couldn't believe what she was seeing. The man that she loved so dearly was lying unconscious on a hospital bed with tubes running from his nose and throat. There was a medley of other tubes running up his arms and across his chest from the pulse heart rate monitor, IV, and other gadgets Simone didn't recognize. Her heart broke into several little pieces. She could never have ever imagined the feeling she was having at that moment. She could feel her heart beating to the rhythm of the loud beeps that were coming from the machines. He was so helpless. A way she had never seen David. Walking over to the bed, she held his hand and kissed it gently. She watched the line on the EKG machine as it too moved to the same rhythm of the beeping sound. David's heartbeat. She prayed the beeps wouldn't stop. With tears still flowing, she continued praying silently, pleading to God: *Lord, please, please spare David's life. You know, Lord, that he's lived his life for you. I know this prayer is so very selfish but please, don't take him from me, God. Not now... Not now...* Simone looked up and noticed that Big Momma and Summer had walked up to the other side of the bed.

Summer leaned over and kissed him. "I love you, Daddy. Please don't leave me." Tears ran down her face. Big Momma wrapped her arm around Summer's shoulder and her other hand laid on David's leg.

The door opened and in walked a tall man in a long white lab coat. "Hello. My name is Dr. Singh." He extended his arm to shake each of their hands.

They each said hello in response.

"I'm one of the doctors that have been caring for Officer McClain. I'm sorry to meet you under such tragic circumstances."

"Likewise," Simone said. "What can you tell us about how David is doing?"

"At this time he is in a medically induced coma. We have him on a ventilator. He is currently unable to breathe on his own. From what we can tell so far, he was shot at least seven times. He suffered severe damage to his lungs from where one of the bullets went through his abdomen. We are also treating a wound in his back where the bullet exited near the thoracic spine. There was damage to the spinal cord. Not to alarm you but I have to tell you, he may be paralyzed."

Simone gasped. Her hand flew to her mouth.

"We're still doing test, and will know a lot more about his condition when we get the results. He's in critical condition; until his status changes, we'll try to make him as comfortable as possible. He will remain in intensive care indefinitely."

There was no hiding Simone's growing concern after hearing David's diagnosis. With an unsteady, quivering voice Simone asked, "Doctor, is he going to make it?"

"It's too soon to tell, but just know that we're doing everything we can to make sure he does."

CHAPTER 7

Summer

SUMMER COULDN'T BELIEVE what she was hearing. *This is not really happening. Is this an awful nightmare? Nightmare! My nightmares always have gunshots in them. My daddy was shot. Oh my God.*

"Baby, what's wrong? You look like you've seen a ghost. What are you thinking about? I can tell by the look on your face that your mind just went somewhere else," Big Momma said.

"Big Momma, do you remember the nightmares I've been having? Remember how I told you the shooting kept happening out of nowhere?"

"Yes, I do remember that."

"You told me that my dreams could be God's way of preparing me for something to come." Her eyes watered. "Do you think God could have been trying to show me that something bad was going to happen to Daddy?"

Big Momma took Summer in her bosom and held her tight. "Baby, He just might have been. I hate to say it but I think so."

Summer started wailing uncontrollably.

Simone came over to help console her. "Sweetie, you're saying you're still having the nightmares?"

She hesitated but she couldn't lie to her mother any longer. "Yes, ma'am."

"Summer."

"Baby, we just have to trust God to see us through this. He knows what He's doing," Big Momma said.

"But Big Momma, why would God let this happen to Daddy? He has never hurt anyone. He always tries to go out of his way to help people, even those most people wouldn't even think about helping."

With watery eyes, Big Momma responded, "Honey, God has a plan for each of our lives. As hard as it is to understand and as painful as it might be, sometimes that even means Him allowing bad things to happen in order for His purpose to be fulfilled. I don't know why He let this happen, but what I do know is that we have to trust and believe that anything that God allows to happen is for a reason. We also have to pray really hard that God's will is to bring your daddy through this."

"I hear what you're saying, Big Momma, and I know you always know what's best. I just don't feel good about this and I want so badly for my daddy to come through this alive." Summer paused. "I really don't understand. I hate to admit it but I'm mad that God would allow something like this to happen to my daddy when there are so many bad people walking around doing all kinds of crazy things. I know I shouldn't question God but I want to know why. Why him?"

"Baby, God has a reason for everything He allows to happen and sometimes we don't understand it but you can bet He knows what He's doing."

The door opened and a police officer walked in followed by a priest.

"Mrs. McClain?" inquired the man in the blue suit.

"Yes? I'm Mrs. McClain." Simone turned around to face the gentlemen.

"Hello, ma'am. I'm Detective Mark Dawson of the Chicago Police Department and this is Father Charles Logan. He's one of the chaplains here at Christ Hospital."

"Hello, ma'am," Father Logan said. "My prayers are with your husband and your family. If there is anything I or anyone here at Christ Hospital can do for you, please don't hesitate to let me know."

"Thank you very much," Simone replied. "This is my daughter, Summer and my mother-in-law, Clara Belle. We call her Big Momma."

"Nice to meet you all. I'm going to leave and let the detective have some time with your family. Know that I'm only a phone call away." He handed Simone a business card.

"Thank you very much, Father."

"You're welcome." Father Logan left and the detective turned his attention to Simone.

"Ma'am, I don't want to take you away from your husband's side for too long, but if it's okay, I'd like to talk to you for a few minutes about what happened to him. Would that be okay?"

"Yes, definitely."

The detective walked over by the window and motioned Simone to follow him. He politely offered a chair to Simone and Big Momma who both sat down. He sat between them while Summer stood.

"There's still a lot of information we don't know yet. What we do know at this time is that Officer McClain was dispatched on a call for a burglary. He was shot in the parking lot after leaving there."

"Where?" Simone questioned.

"He was at The Towers and was shot outside the home where he made the run."

"Do you know who did this and why?" Simone pleaded.

"No. At this time we have no leads. We've been keeping the area flooded with officers and we've been asking around but no one is talking. Everyone is saying they didn't see anything. Unfortunately, people in the streets have this attitude of 'don't snitch.'"

"Just a shame, Jesus. A crying shame." Big Momma shook her head.

"Well, shouldn't another officer have seen what happened? Wasn't someone with him? Where was his partner, Jay?" Simone asked.

"We've talked to Officer Lopez. The call came through at lunch time. He said he was getting ready to leave for a doctor's appointment and your husband didn't think taking a simple report was worth him changing his appointment, so he went alone. Officer Lopez is taking this very hard. He blames himself. He's saying he should have been there to help him."

"Why would someone do this to David? Why?" Simone wept.

"I'm sorry." Detective Dawson reached for a box of tissue sitting on the window sill and handed it to Simone. "At this time we're still trying to do all that we can to find out more about what happened and who was involved. Please trust that we're going to do everything in our power to find out who did this. We don't take an officer being shot lightly."

As the detective continued speaking, the door opened. It was Jay.

He looks like he's been hit by a semi. Summer had never seen him look that way. His hair was messy, his uniform shirt was hanging out and not neatly tucked in like usual, and his eyes were bloodshot red. Summer could tell that he had been crying. This was not the Uncle Jay she was used to seeing. He was always very clean cut and neat which made him look even more handsome. The detective was right. He was taking this as hard as they were.

"Hello, Simone. Summer. Big Momma."

"Hello, Jay." Simone went over and hugged him.

"Hi, baby," Big Momma said. Jay was the other son she never had.

"Hi, Uncle Jay." Summer walked over and gave him a hug.

They all loved Jay and considered him to be part of the family. It certainly felt like he was. The number of years that he and David had been best friends and partners brought them all together. He came to the house periodically for dinner and has never missed a holiday.

"Detective Dawson was just talking to us about what happened to David. It sounds like there are still a lot of missing pieces," Simone said.

"Yes, there is, but I promise you that the thugs who did this to David are going to be found. I promise you that. Even if I have to find them all by myself," Jay stated.

"Officer. We appreciate your help, but you really have to let the process work."

Jay huffed. "Process?"

Detective Dawson stood up. "Will you all please excuse us for a moment?"

"Sure." Simone looked concerned for Jay.

The detective walked toward Jay and touched him on the arm, indicating that he'd like him to go with him. Jay pulled his arm away. The detective looked at him a moment, then walked toward the door. Jay followed him outside the door, away from the family. Although the detective was trying to whisper, Summer could still make out what he was saying.

"Officer Lopez, I understand that you are emotionally connected to this case. However, this is still official police business. You can't allow your feelings to interfere with the investigation."

"Detective Dawson," Jay responded. "I understand full well that this is *official* police business, but you know what? Let's be clear. That's *my* partner lying in that bed in there all shot up with wires running all over his body. That's *my* best friend. So while you all are trying to do your *official* police business, if you don't find out *real* fast who's responsible for this happening to him, I will find out myself and that's a promise you can take to the bank. What I can't promise is that when I do find them, and I will find them Detective, I won't promise you that I'll be following *official* police procedures."

"Officer Lopez, will you please lower your voice?"

"Is there anything else, Detective?"

"Please let us do our job. I understand how you feel, but we have to do this the right way."

"Detective, let me ask you a question. Has your partner and best friend ever been gunned down and you were not there to help him when you should have been?"

Detective Dawson stuttered, "No—No. I haven't."

"Well, Detective, you have no idea how I feel."

The door opened and Jay walked back into the room. Detective Dawson followed behind him but stayed near the door. Summer, Simone, and Big Momma began making small talk with one another in an attempt to look like they hadn't heard their conversation. Jay walked over to David's bed and looked at David for a few minutes.

Summer realized how her heart ached for her dad, but it now ached for Jay. She could see that he was not only filled with pain but also with guilt. She wished that there was something she could do or say that would make him feel better.

"Man, I'm so sorry I wasn't there with you on that run." Tears were filling his eyes. He looked exhausted. "I'm sorry this happened to you. Please pull through this, David. We've been through a lot, man. I need you to come through this, too. I swear on my life that I'm going to find out who did this to you. I swear. I love you, man." He put his fist up to David's hand. Then he walked away from the bed and over to Simone. "Simone. I love you. I'm really sorry about this."

"Jay, this isn't your fault. Please don't blame yourself."

"I've gotta go. Please call me if you need anything. You know how to reach me."

"We love you, too, Jay. Please take care of yourself."

"I will. I'm going to go. I'll see you all later." He walked out the door with his head hanging.

CHAPTER 8

Simone

A WEEK HAD gone by and the investigation had still not moved forward. Simone was very frustrated that the police department had not identified any suspects. David still had not shown any progress in spite of the fact that he had undergone several surgeries. The doctors confirmed that he had been shot a total of ten times. The surgeons were successful in removing nine of the bullets but couldn't remove the last one because it was near his heart. It was too risky to chance.

Simone had been by his side every day around the clock. She was exhausted but refused to leave his side except to get something to eat or to take a shower. Dr. Singh told her it would probably be a while before there was a change in David's status. He told her that if she wanted to go home to get some rest she could and the hospital would call her if there were any changes.

"I appreciate your offer, Doctor, but there's no way I'm leaving my husband's side. I want him to know I'm here when he wakes up." She didn't care how long she had to take showers in the hospital's guest room area or sleeping in David's room in the chair. There was no doubt in her mind that if the tables were turned, David would be right there by her side and there wouldn't be anyone on this earth that would have been able to get him to leave her. Their relationship had always been one of loyalty and they'd always been inseparable. Simone wasn't about to let that change now when David needed her most.

Simone sat watching David. Her heart was filled with so much pain as she peered at him lying helplessly and knowing she was unable to help him. It had been absolute torture. "David, you wouldn't imagine the emotional roller coaster I've been on this last week. I've been hurt, afraid, and angry all at the same time. But mostly I've been afraid. I know it sounds selfish but..." She sniffled and wiped her nose with a tissue. "I've been afraid I'll have to live without you." Tears poured. "I could never imagine a life where you don't exist, David. You're our world. Mine, Summer's, and Big Momma's. I just want everything to be back to normal. I feel so helpless. You know I'm used to being in control of everything and being able to fix whatever is broken. I'm lost, babe. For the first time in my life, I can't fix what is wrong." She sat and wept for a few minutes. "You know, David, I wish I was able to lie in my mother's arms or hold my daddy's hand, and for them to tell me that everything is going to be okay." That's exactly what they would have been doing if she hadn't told them not to make the long trip just yet from San Antonio. They were getting up in age and she knew the long drive would be taxing on them. She'd preferred that they flew when they came to visit but there was no way anyone would ever get either of them on an airplane. She had to rely on her faith. She always had trusted God, but for the first time ever, she had to put complete faith in Him. She talked to Him like never before.

She bowed her head and began to pray: *God, I feel like all I've done in the past week is ask You to do things for me. I am thankful for all You've ever done in my life but I'm coming to You again. I'm asking You, Lord, please let David show some sign of life. Spare his life, Lord so that he can continue to do Your work. I ask this in Your precious Son, Jesus' name. Amen.* Any little sign at that time would have given her a glimmer of hope. The wait was agonizing. Not to mention she felt deep loneliness. In seventeen years, that had been the longest she had ever gone without communicating with David. It felt awkward not talking to him, laughing, hearing him say 'good night' and 'I love you' before they went to bed at night. She closed her eyes and imagined they were at home and everything was okay again. She pleaded to God one last time. *Lord. Please let him wake up.*

CHAPTER 9

Summer

During the week and a half since her dad had been shot, Summer had been a nervous wreck. She had felt a small sense of relief because the doctors decided to take her dad out of the medically induced coma. His vital signs had begun to show signs of improvement. His respirations and heart rate were steady enough that they were confident he could breathe on his own. They removed the breathing tube from his throat so that he might be able to speak if he woke up.

Summer and Simone sat silently next to one another. Both of them were grateful for just a little bit of improvement.

Summer's phone rang and distracted her from her thoughts. It had to be Jasmine.

She had been calling her constantly since the accident and had also been coming by her house regularly to see if she needed anything. Summer really appreciated the love Jasmine was showing her during the most difficult time of her life. She took her phone from her pocket and looked at the screen to see whose number was on the display, and then pushed the green talk button.

"Hey, Jazz." After waiting a few minutes she responded. "He's still not conscious but the doctors said that he's doing better and they've taken the tube out of his throat. We're just praying that he'll wake up soon." She paused. "Okay. I'll talk to you later. Thanks. Bye." She disconnected the call.

"How's Jazz doing?" Simone said.

"She's fine. She was just checking on me again. She's been blowing up my phone." Thinking of Jasmine made her smile. Something she hadn't done in the past week and a half.

"She really is a good friends. Her and Antoine. You know you're very blessed to have them both, right?"

"I know." She smiled again.

"Baby, Big Momma said she was on her way here. She should be here any time now. I think I'll go down and meet her as she comes in and grab me a bite to eat in the cafeteria while I'm down there. Do you want to go with me?"

"No, ma'am. I ate before I left home. You know Big Momma. She's been worried about me. She's been making sure that I've been eating every single meal and then some." They laughed.

"Okay. You sure you don't want me to bring you anything? Not even a small snack?"

"No, ma'am. Thanks anyway."

"Okay. I'll be right back."

Summer walked over to her dad's bed and held his hand. It comforted her to feel close to him. She had never been more afraid in her entire life. Her daddy was the person who always made her feel safe. It didn't seem real that she was standing there watching him lie helpless in a hospital bed. She sniffled as a tear fell down her face. Her heart ached. She closed her eyes and prayed silently. *God, please. Please help Daddy to wake up. I need him so much. I don't know what I'd do without him.*

She heard a groan. She slowly opened her eyes. David's eyes were closed but his head moved slightly from side to side. He groaned again.

"Daddy!"

His eyes were still closed. "Summer?" David whispered, groggily.

"Yes, Daddy. It's me, Summer." Tears slowly fell from her eyes.

Still whispering, he managed to say, "Where am I?" He touched the IV on his arm and felt the tubes on his chest. "What's all this stuff on me?" Slowly he opened his eyes.

"Daddy, you were shot." She was so happy he was awake. Happy to look into his eyes, but she didn't know what to do. She didn't want to leave him but at the same time she thought she should call for the doctor. She also knew that the police was anxious to speak with him. She couldn't think straight.

"Summer. Where is your mom?"

That's a good question. Where is she and what is taking her so long? "Daddy, she'll be right back. She went to meet Big Momma and to get something to eat. I'm not sure you should be talking." *The buzzer. I can buzz the doctor.* "Maybe I should call the doctor." She reached for the call button on his bed.

His grip tightened on her hand. "Summer, listen." He began breathing harder. He sounded very tired.

"Yes, Daddy?"

"I love you, your mother, and Big Momma very much. I don't know if I'm going to make it through this."

"Daddy, please stop. Don't say that." More tears began to flood her eyes.

"Please don't worry about me. I'm going to be okay, and I want you, your mother, and Big Momma to be okay. Tell them I love them."

"Daddy, I told you, Mom is coming right back. You can tell her yourself."

He began to talk slower. "Listen to me, Summer. You're growing up to be a beautiful young lady. Inside and out. I want you to know how proud I am of you." Summer cried harder and just nodded her head.

"Always remember that God has a purpose for your life. Live for God and know that there's a whole world out here that is waiting to be touched by you. Whatever you choose to do with your life, make sure it's what you want to do…as… long as you live with…" He coughed then continued, "…a purpose. Make a difference. Do not let my life be in vain."

"What do you mean, Daddy?"

David began coughing. He was still trying to talk but his whisper was so low that it came out as mumbling. Summer couldn't understand what he was saying. He coughed again.

"Daddy, don't talk anymore. I'm going to call the nurse." She reached for the call button and pushed it. David was still coughing.

"Where are they?" Summer said. The minute that passed felt like hours. The door opened and in rushed a nurse, another man that appeared to be a doctor, and Dr. Singh. They pushed Summer out of the way and began checking David's pulse, then immediately put an oxygen mask over his mouth.

Shortly after they began working on him, Simone and Big

Momma walked in. Summer began to explain. "Mom, Daddy woke up."

"What's going on? Is he okay?" Simone asked.

"Ma'am, he's regained consciousness. At this time we're checking his vitals. His breathing is labored. We're giving him oxygen hoping to improve it," Dr. Singh said.

The door opened again and in walked Detective Dawson. "I noticed all the commotion coming toward this room and asked one of the doctors what was going on. I understand Officer McClain is conscious. Doctor, can I have a few minutes with him? It's imperative that we speak with him right away."

"Detective, I'm sorry, but this is not the time. Right now he's not strong enough to talk and we need to make sure his vitals stay stable now that he is conscious. As soon as he's strong enough, we'll let you know."

"Do you know when that might be? We don't want to lose any time." He glanced at Simone, Big Momma, and Summer, then continued speaking to the doctor in a lower voice. "Or the opportunity to speak with him, given the situation." Summer was disturbed by his comment. Her concerned look turned into a frown.

"I can't give you a definite time," Dr. Singh said.

"If you could just—"

"Detective, if you can't tell, my husband is fighting for his life here. I appreciate what you're trying to do but now isn't a good time," Simone said.

"I...I understand." Detective Dawson stepped back towards the door.

Summer turned her attention to the other doctor and the nurses that were still working on her dad who was looking at

Big Momma. Then he turned his eyes to Simone. He reached toward her. He coughed harder and louder. Blood began to seep from his mouth and run down the side of his face.

Summer screamed, "Daddy!"

The nurses removed the mask. "Turn him on his side so he won't choke on his blood," she insisted.

"Everyone. Out! Now!" Dr. Singh yelled. He gave the detective a very stern look and turned his attention to Summer, Simone, and Big Momma. Lowering his voice he said, "I'm very sorry. We need to get him back to surgery right away. It appears that he's having internal bleeding. We need to find the source of the bleeding, immediately."

Now crying herself, Simone responded, "Yes, Doctor. Please take care of him. We don't want to lose him."

Dr. Singh nodded his head slightly and gave a small smile, then turned and went back to David.

Big Momma looked at David and said, "Baby, you're in God's hands. I love you with all of my heart."

"I love you, Daddy," Summer yelled.

Backing out the door Simone looked at David and spoke lightly, "I love you, honey."

Lying on his side, he just stared at them. His eyes said he loved them too.

SIMONE, Summer, and Big Momma sat alone, anxiously but quietly in the waiting room for news of how David was doing. After they prayed together, Simone turned to Summer.

"Summer, were you in the room the whole time I was gone?"

"Yes, ma'am."

"Were you there when your dad woke up?"

Summer's thoughts drifted to what Dr. Singh said. *I'm sorry, but right now he's not strong enough to talk.* But her daddy had talked. *Had he talked too much? Is that what made him start coughing?* "Yes, Mom. I was there when he woke up. He talked to me."

"He talked to you?"

"Yes. I told him that I wasn't sure if he should be talking and tried to call the doctor but he grabbed my arm and stopped me. It was hard to hear him but he kept talking like he really had to tell me something."

What did he say?"

"He was just telling me that he loved us and he wanted us to be okay. He wanted me to tell you all that he loved you. He told me how proud he was of me and he said he didn't know if he was going to make it through this. That really worried me. Then right before he started coughing he said something." Summer stopped.

"What did he say?"

Summer could still hear his weak voice saying, *Do not let my life be in vain.* But she didn't want to repeat it. It sounded so final. Why wasn't he sure he'd pull through this? She needed him to pull through, and what did it mean anyway?

"What did he say, Summer?"

"He said for me not to let his life be in vain. It's like he was telling me there was something he wanted me to do but wasn't saying what it was." Her eyes were watering and she became overcome by fear.

"Sometimes people talk in riddles when they come out of a coma. They don't realize what they're saying."

"Yeah, but Daddy seemed very clear on what he was saying. It's almost as if he was saying goodbye."

Big Momma embraced Summer. "Baby, your daddy is in God's hands. He won't let anything happen to him that He doesn't intend to happen. We know He can perform miracles that will leave us amazed. None of us are going to leave this earth until God says it's time."

"But what did he mean about me not letting his life be in vain?"

"Baby, either your daddy will tell you when he gets better, or God will have to put it on your heart when the time is right. Neither your mother or I can really tell you that."

Summer looked at her mom for confirmation. Simone nodded in agreement.

Frustrated, Summer retreated back to the seat on the couch feeling defeated. She needed to talk to him. He would tell her what he meant. She decided not to worry about it for the time being. She wanted to believe that her daddy was going to come out of surgery successfully and they would all be at home again soon, sitting around the table, eating Big Momma's food, laughing and joking.

Two hours passed and they were still waiting. Jay had returned to the hospital and Pastor Morris, the family's pastor, was there as well. Everyone's frustration of having to wait was apparent. Jay was pacing the floor. Summer was trying to watch the TV but couldn't concentrate, while Big Momma and Simone sat trying to make conversation. Pastor Morris would periodically say something inspirational, trying to keep everyone at peace.

After another hour, Dr. Singh finally walked in followed by Father Logan.

"Father Logan? We… We didn't expect to see you today. Doctor? How's David? Is he in his room resting? Can we see him now? How did—"

"Mrs. McClain. I'm so sorry to have to tell you this but… Mr. McClain didn't make it."

"Noooooo," Summer yelled. "I want my daddy. I want my daddy." She fell against the wall and began pleading, "God please. Not my daddy." She felt a stab of resentment and turned toward the doctor in rage. "You were supposed to save him." She slid down to the floor where she sat and cried.

Simone fell to her knees in the praying position and tears were pouring from her eyes. "Lord, no. Please tell me this isn't true. Lord, please. Please."

Big Momma just stood in place, strong like the soldier she was, with her eyes closed and her head pointed up.

"Lord. My son is with You now. With a heavy, heavy heart, I trust that Your will has been done. Please Lord, help my family to get through this like only You can. I give it all to You, Lord."

Father Logan walked over to Simone and helped her off the floor. Holding her by her arm, he helped her over to the couch.

Pastor Morris consoled Simone. When she seemed to have gotten her composure Dr. Singh continued, "We tried for almost three hours to stop the bleeding that we found to have been coming from his lungs. They collapsed, which caused the bleeding from his mouth and the chest pains he was experiencing. We tried very hard. I am so sorry but we couldn't save him."

Detective Dawson walked into the waiting room observing how upset everyone was.

He asked Dr. Singh, "Is he unconscious again? How bad is his condition?"

"I'm sorry, Detective, but Mr. McClain passed away."

"Oh, no." He dropped his head. He turned to the family and began walking toward Simone. Jay stepped in front of him, stopping him in his tracks. Jay had been silent since Dr. Singh gave them the news.

"Detective, this is personal now. I'm going to say this one last time and I won't say it again. You better find who killed David and I guarantee you, you don't have a whole lot of time to do it. If you don't find them soon, I will." Before the detective could respond Jay turned and walked out.

CHAPTER 10

Summer

Summer reached her arm out and slammed her hand on the snooze button once again. Her alarm was going off for the fifth time in the past forty-five minutes. She lay back on her pillow and went back to staring at the ceiling. No matter how hard she tried, she could not drag herself out of bed on this particular day. It was the day she had been dreading for the past four days and it had finally come. It was the day of her father's funeral. The more she considered getting out of bed, the more anxiety grew inside of her. The past four days had been completely miserable but nothing could compare to how she felt right then. She didn't know how she would say goodbye. She didn't want to say goodbye. The fear, anger, and pain continued to rise with every passing moment. She lay there thinking about how nothing in her life would ever be the same again. In a single moment and with one stupid decision, someone that she didn't even know had changed her life forever.

She was startled from her thoughts by a soft knock on the door. "Come in."

"Good morning, honey."

"Good morning, Mom."

Simone walked over to the bed and sat on the edge. She reached over on the nightstand and turned off the clock. Then she reached for her daughter's hand and rubbed it.

"Baby, it's time to get up. We're going to have to get this day started sooner or later."

"I know, Mom." Summer felt like grabbing her sheet and pulling it over her head. She kept hoping that she would wake up and things would be back to normal, but she knew that wasn't possible. Unlike the nightmares that had been haunting her over the past month, this one was real.

"I'm getting ready to get up. I don't want to, though. This is the worst day of my life."

"I know, honey. Mine too, but we have to face it at some time. We'll have to take comfort in the fact that your daddy is looking down on us from heaven and although we don't have him here physically to protect us anymore he's now our guardian angel."

Summer, Simone, Simone's parents, Big Momma, and Jay rode to the church silently in the limousine. Summer stared out the window, still in disbelief. *How could this be happening to me? How am I going to make it without my daddy, one of the people that I love more than anything in this entire world?* Tears were running down her cheeks as they had been for the past week. Unless somehow a person was capable of running out of tears, Summer didn't know if hers would ever stop. Frankly, she didn't care.

As the limousine turned onto the street where the First Ebenezer Missionary Church sat, Summer noticed that cars were parked blocks away. The parking lot had no spaces available. The entire perimeter of the church had police cars all around it.

The limousine pulled up to the front of the church in the space that was reserved. They were escorted inside by the funeral home personnel. Summer couldn't believe her eyes as she entered the vestibule and peered into the church. She turned to Simone, "Mom, I knew Daddy was loved but this is unbelievable. There are hundreds of people out here to pay their respects to him. That is way cool."

Simone smiled. "Yes, baby. It is way cool. I'm not surprised. Your daddy touched the lives of so many people. He was very loved and respected and he deserves the most wonderful home-going service possible."

"Your daddy always did know how to touch people in a way that others couldn't," Big Momma said.

Simone nodded then looked at Summer. "Are you ready to do this?"

Taking a deep breath Summer responded, "As ready as I'll ever be." She took another deep breath and began to walk. Her legs became numb as she walked down the aisle. Somehow she managed to continue moving.

The ushers escorted them to the row that was reserved for the family in the front of the church where they sat in front of David's casket. The foot of his casket had an American flag draped over it. One-by-one they went up to view David's body. When Summer walked up to the casket, the reality finally settled in that these really were the final moments that she would ever have with her father. She broke down crying harder than she had since they first heard the news. It didn't seem real watching him lie stiff on the white satin cloth that reminded her of white clouds. Big Momma and Simone came to console her and to help her back to her seat.

Finally, she was able to get her composure enough to address people as they came by to pay their respects. Hundreds of people came up to offer their condolences. Many told them they were keeping the family in their prayers and offered to help in various ways. Others offered fond memories of times they had shared with David and how wonderful they thought he was.

There were so many people there that Summer knew and many more that she didn't know at all. She knew members of the Chicago Police Department would be there, but she had no idea that they would come out in such large numbers. It looked as if the entire department was there along with the fire department, state police, and the sheriff's department, to say goodbye to her daddy. Big Momma introduced Simone and Summer to lots of people that David had been friends with in high school and college. Two men and two women approached the family in a group. They stopped and three of them talked to Simone for several minutes. Finally, the tall, slender woman that had been silent must have detected that Simone couldn't place them.

"Hi, Simone." She took Simone's hand in hers and held it tightly.

"Hello. This is my daughter, Summer."

"You're beautiful. You look just like your dad. I'm Michelle. This is Johnny, Stacey, and Kyle." They shook Simone and Summer's hands.

"Simone, you remember them. David's friends from college, the one's that he told you used to come home with him on weekends," Big Momma chimed in.

Michelle continued, "Big Momma, we still remember those good meals you used to make for us. Simone, it's been quite a few years since we met you."

Johnny jumped in, "Yeah. We hadn't seen David in a while. You know. Life got busy for all of us."

"Remember how proud David was of his new lady friend and how excited he was when he told us about Simone?"

"Oh my gosh, yes. David talked about you so much shortly after you two started dating. He couldn't wait to introduce you to us. We were so excited when we finally met you at your wedding. You made David so happy and we were happy for you both," Michelle continued.

"Yes, I do remember you guys. There were so many people at our wedding. David was crazy about you all. He always spoke very highly of you all and talked a lot about the great times you all used to have together." Simone now recalled.

"We definitely had some good times," Kyle remembered.

Stacey said, "We had never seen David so happy. We had no doubt that he had found his soul mate. He loved you so much."

"Thank you all for being here. It means so much."

"There's no way we wouldn't have been here," Michelle said. "Although we hadn't seen David in a while, we still loved him like a brother. Like Kyle said," she turned and pointed toward him, "we've all kind of been doing our own thing over the years. It's unfortunate that it took losing him to bring us all back together." They looked around at one another with looks of shame on their faces.

"But we're going to do better. David would want us to," Johnny vowed.

Michelle spoke for the group again, "Let us know if there is anything we can do for you all."

"Thank you," Simone said.

After the four of them moved on to their seats, others continued to come by and express their condolences. There were people David knew throughout the community, school, church, and various other places throughout Chicago. The family continued to show their gratitude.

Simone greeted several of her own friends that she had not seen in many years. As always, Vivian was right there by her side showing her support.

There were hundreds of students that were there to show their respects. Summer was surprised to see that even Monique and her crew of Raquel and Macy showed up. Of course her best friends, Jasmine and Antoine, were right by her side. Their parents were sitting a few rows behind the family. There were teachers there, some that had taught her and many that had not. There were administrators and other faculty present as well. She didn't realize she was even noticed enough by so many people that they would take the time out to come for her father's funeral. She always spoke to people, but really only had a small group of friends that she dealt with. She figured by now, many of them recognized her father as the officer that worked at the school but none of them mentioned it if they did.

Dr. Singh, Father Logan, and many of the doctors and nurses at the hospital that had cared for David even showed up. She was definitely touched by their kindness.

She began to feel very uneasy. *There are more faces that I don't recognize here than those that I do. I wonder if Daddy's killer could be right here at the funeral.* She began looking around the church randomly picking out people that now looked suspicious. Her mind was going wild as one face after the other began appearing to be the killer flashing through her mind. Suddenly the room felt like it was spinning. It was tearing her up inside.

"Praise God."

Distracted by the voice of Pastor Morris, who was now standing in the pulpit at the podium, Summer looked up at him and blinked her eyes. She was trying to gain focus. She lightly shook her head hoping to shake the visions of her dad's potential killers from her mind.

The services were about to begin and people were wrapping up their individual conversations and scurrying to get to their seats.

Pastor Morris stood tall and repeated, "Praise God everyone."

"Praise God," the crowd responded. The church fell silent.

"At this time our amazing choir will minister to you in song." The choir stood and sang several songs including *His Eye is On the Sparrow* and Boys2Men's *It's So Hard To Say Goodbye To Yesterday*. The crowd cried and clapped as they stood with their hands raised high. When they were done and seated Pastor Morris returned to the podium.

"Thank you, choir for those wonderful songs. Brothers and sisters, today we are gathered here to honor the life and legacy of a true and faithful servant of God, Brother David McClain. I, like all of you, are going to truly miss Brother David."

"Yes, Lord," a lady yelled.

Pastor Morris went on to introduce several people, mostly preachers, who all were scheduled to speak about David's life for two minutes. Very few of them followed instructions and stayed within their allotted two minutes. Every time one went over their time limit, it seemed the next one tried to outdo the last one. They all had great things to say about their experiences with David and their memories of him. When Jay spoke to the crowd about his special times with David it seemed to have been the most stirring moment of the entire service. As he was speaking, Summer didn't think he would be able to finish because he was so broken up but he managed to get through his two minute speech. His words really touched her.

"Every moment we spent working together, laughing together, debating with one another, and just sharing the things that mattered most to us, will forever be imbedded in my heart. I'm a better person because David McClain lived in this world. My life will have a void that can never be filled now that he is no longer here. He was my partner. He was my friend. He was my brother, and he will forever be loved and missed."

The crowd was noticeably moved by Jay's words and his deep felt emotions. It was strange seeing Jay in this way. He was always happy go lucky. Zoe waited as he returned to his seat to comfort him.

Pastor Morris stood to begin his eulogy. "It's obvious from the outpouring of love and kind words that we just heard from everyone that Brother David made an impact on everyone whose life he touched. You know? When I heard the news that he didn't make it, like many of you, I thought in the natural sense. A great man snatched away too soon. But brothers and sisters, God quickly reminded me that although it may seem that way, God knows what he's doing. Before David was even a seed in his mother's womb, God knew the day, the time, and the way he would leave this earth. And even before he was a seed in his mother's womb, God had a plan for his life. Brother David, he was truly a light for the world to see. And you know the thing that I always noticed? No matter where I'd see him, he was always the same. Many times I'd see him in his uniform working on the streets of Chicago. He was exactly the same man that he was when I'd see him in his suit and tie on Sunday morning. He'd be serving the Lord and talking to a young person about what they could potentially be. And he didn't do it as a show for me because I'm the pastor either. I've heard many people say the same thing about Brother David."

"Amen," a lady shouted.

"God had a true anointing on his life. Like David in the Bible. He wasn't perfect. He made mistakes like we all do, but he was a man of God's own heart. His life was purposed to be a warrior for Christ. That's exactly what Brother David was. The name David means beloved one. When you look at the man King David was in the Bible and his character, you see that he was a man that truly loved God. He knew that anything that was contrary to the will of God was also contrary to the *word* of God. Whenever King David felt he had traveled within those boundaries that didn't include God he would do whatever…I said whatever!"

"Whatever," a man yelled.

"He'd do whatever it took to make it right with God. David was a repenting man. He'd make it right. So would our Brother David McClain. He lived his life for Christ. He always made sure he was in God's will. And he didn't make any apologies about it. He loved the Lord. He has made his mark on us Brothers and Sisters. Let's not let his legacy be in vain."

Do not let my life be in vain. Summer could hear her father's voice say.

Pastor Morris continued. "Continue to do the works that Brother David started. Remember the lessons he taught us all, to love each other. To believe in one another no matter how things may look like on the surface. To be able to see that diamond in the rough and to polish it so that it shines. He taught us that we have to go on and to never give up on life, because God has a purpose for each one of our lives."

You have to go on because God has a purpose for each one of our lives. Summer could hear her father's voice again. Those were the same words he'd told her after Megan committed suicide.

Pastor Morris preached on. "The days that follow are going to be tough for you, McClain family, friends, and all those that loved Brother David. It may not seem like it now but you will get through it. Remember his legacy, to change the world starting right here in the community of Chicago. He will always be remembered as a great and loving husband, father, son, friend, and co-worker. He'll be remembered as the person you want to be around because his heart was so pure. Will you let his life and legacy be in vain? What will your legacy be? Will people remember you because you were a good person that tried to change the world? When you're gone, brothers and sisters, people won't remember the kind of car you drove or how big your house was. Or what kind of executive job you had. Or how much money you had. What they will remember is how you treated them. How you made them feel. The impact you made on this earth. So, brothers and sisters, I ask you again, what will your legacy be? To the McClain family, your hearts are heavy with pain today. It's okay to cry. It may be hard to imagine this now, but your pain will get lighter. The Good Book tells us in Psalm thirtieth chapter, fifth verse that weeping may endure for a night, but joy comes in the morning. What will last forever is the great memories and the love you have for Brother David. On behalf of First Ebenezer Missionary Church, thank you for allowing us the privilege and honor of taking part in the farewell services for the man of God. Family, if we can do anything to help you through your mourning process and thereafter, please let us know. As your church family, we love you and we are here for you. Always. God bless each and every one of you." The choir began to sing *I'll Fly Away* as the casket was carried out of the church. The family followed behind and the people filed out.

The service lasted for a little over an hour. David's farewell ended at the graveyard. The rest of the day went by like a blur. Summer barely registered the pomp and circumstance around her. She did recall that after Pastor Morris said his final words of comfort to the family and friends of David, seventeen white doves were released and flew into the sky.

"Each dove represents one of the years that Brother David McClain dedicated his life to service on the Chicago Police Department," Pastor Morris said.

My life will never, ever be the same again. Summer knew that she would never ever be able to get past the pain and the anger she currently felt. She swallowed hard. For that moment she tried to push past her pain and tears and imagine as she watched the beautiful white doves flying in the sky that she could see her daddy peeking through the clouds smiling at her, winking his eye, wearing his new angel wings.

CHAPTER 11

Summer

THE DAYS THAT followed David's funeral were agonizing and lonely. Although everyone was there, the house felt empty and cold. They all grieved in their own way. Summer stayed to herself, confined in her bedroom with her iPod and the telephone for when Jasmine called. She was tired of looking at TV. The more she watched, the more depressed she felt. No matter what channel she turned to, there was a report about her father's murder.

"*The murderer of police officer David McClain is still at large. The suspect is considered armed and dangerous. Officer McClain was gunned down at The Towers projects and later died at the hospital. No word has been given from the Chicago Police Department if a suspect has been named.*"

Another station reported, "*No suspect has been named yet in the murder investigation of seventeen year veteran police officer, David McClain, who was gunned down in the line of duty less than three weeks ago and later died at Christ Hospital.*"

She picked up the remote control and pushed the power

button turning off the TV. She couldn't take it anymore. It just made her too sad to relive the whole nightmare of her father being murdered over and over again.

I'm thirsty. She dropped the remote control on her bed, stood up, and stuck her feet in her house shoes. She headed toward the kitchen. When she stepped into the family room, Big Momma was sitting in her favorite chair with her Bible open in her lap. Her head was down and her eyes were closed. She appeared to have been praying but Summer realized that she was crying also. Summer thought about going over to console her but decided against it. *Maybe she needs this time alone.* She turned around and went back to her bedroom. The glass of Hi-C fruit punch could wait.

It was strange seeing Big Momma cry. Of them all, Big Momma had been the one that had shown the most strength through this entire tragedy. She always did. Summer noticed that ever since the funeral, Big Momma had not been able to sit still. If she wasn't cleaning, she was cooking or trying to make sure Summer and Simone were eating. Summer hadn't thought much about it because those were things Big Momma always did, but now she was doing them constantly since David's death. Now Summer wondered if that wasn't Big Momma's way of grieving. Maybe she cried all the time when they weren't around.

Her mother confined herself to her bedroom, lying in the bed for the past several days except for going to the restroom or eating. Summer believed the only reason she ate was because Big Momma insisted. Whenever they sat at the table to eat, Simone sat quietly and picked over her food. To Summer's surprise, she did leave one day, but only because Vivian came over and insisted she get dressed and go with her to dinner and a movie. Simone resisted but Vivian wouldn't take no for an answer. Vivian even combed Simone's hair and helped her get dressed. As soon as Vivian brought her home, Simone went right back to her bedroom and closed the door.

Summer went back to her room again and listened to her iPod while she waited for the phone to ring. She looked at the clock. It was 2:30 p.m. *Jazz and Ms. V. should be home soon from Jasmine's grandmother's house.* Summer understood how her mother felt. She wanted to be left alone, too, for the most part, but she did find talking to Jasmine helped her feel less lonely.

The phone rang and she reached over and grabbed it.

"May I speak with Mrs. McClain?"

Dang, Summer thought as soon as she heard the male voice through the receiver. She had forgotten to look at the caller ID. Knowing it was too late, she looked at the display anyway. It read: *Chicago Police Department.* The detectives on her father's case had been calling their house non-stop for the past several days. Simone had not been up to talking to them yet and had been avoiding their calls. Summer and Big Momma had been screening the calls until Simone gave them the okay that she wanted to talk to them. Summer didn't know what to say so she said the first thing that came to her mind.

"I'm sorry. She's not here right now."

"Do you know when she's expected to return?"

"No. I'm sorry. I don't."

"Well, this is Sergeant Tooley of the Chicago Police Department. I'm now heading up the investigation of Officer McClain. I'll be working very closely with Detective Dawson.

It's imperative that we speak with her. We have a few questions for her as we progress in the investigation."

"Okay. I will let her know when she gets home."

"Thank you. I appreciate it. And who am I speaking to?"

"This is her daughter, Summer."

"Okay, Summer. Thank you very much for passing on my message to your mom."

"You're welcome. Bye."

"Bye."

She placed the phone on the receiver. *Dang! How could I forget to check the caller ID?*

Before she could remove her hand, the phone rang again. This time she remembered to look.

Victoria Michaels came across the display.

"Hey, Jazz."

"Hey, Summer. What are you doing?"

"Just hung up from an investigator with the police department. They keep calling and my mom isn't ready to talk to them yet. I got caught slipping and answered the phone."

"Well, maybe they'll stop calling for a while."

"I hope so."

"Hey, do you want to go to Di Maio's?"

"Well…"

"Come on, Summer. You haven't been out of the house since your dad's funeral. You need to get out."

"Jazz, I really don't feel like it." Now she was wishing she hadn't answer Jasmine's call. She knew how Jasmine hated taking no for an answer.

"Girl, come on. Call Antoine and we can all hang out. Like we used to do."

Hmmm, Antoine. The mention of him reminded her that she hadn't spoken to him since she saw him at her dad's funeral.

He hadn't answered any of her phone calls since then either. "I haven't talked to Antoine."

"You haven't?"

"Nope. Not since the quick hello we said to each other at Daddy's funeral. There were so many people there, I didn't get to talk to either one of you that much. But I've been calling him and he hasn't answered or returned any of my calls."

"That's weird. Well, try to call him again and if you can't get him then we'll go anyway."

Realizing that Jasmine wasn't going to give up, Summer responded, "I guess, Jazz. I'll go for a little while."

"Cool! What time are you picking me up?"

"Give me thirty minutes. And be ready. You know you're never ready when I get there. I get sick of waiting on you."

"Okay, okay. I'll be ready. I'll talk to you later."

"Bye."

Summer disconnected the call. She dialed Antoine's number once again. After four rings it went to his voicemail. She waited for the beep.

"Antoine, this is Summer, again. Jazz and I are going to Di Maio's and wanted to know if you wanted to go with us. I've called you several times and you haven't returned my calls. I'm starting to worry about you. Call me when you get this message." She laid the phone on the receiver.

What's going on with Antoine? He always calls me back. Pushing the thought of him in the back of her mind, she walked over to her dresser and grabbed her brush and pulled her hair back into a ponytail. She slipped on her sandals. "Mom?" She waited a few minutes. There was no response. "Big Momma?"

"Yes, baby?" Big Momma stuck her head out the kitchen door.

"Mom must have not heard me calling her. Jazz wants me to hang out with her at Di Maio's. Is it okay?"

"I think it'll be good for you to get out the house, baby. Have a good time."

"Thanks, Big Momma. I'll see you later." She grabbed her keys and headed out the door.

"Okay, okay. I'll be ready. I'll talk to you later." Finished with her conversation with Summer, Jasmine hung up the phone. She reached down and pulled open her nightstand drawer and pulled out a package of Oreo cookies. She stuffed them in her mouth one by one until she devoured half the pack. She washed them down with milk.

She was still thinking about how sad Summer sounded and how awful she felt for her. She knew how much Summer loved her dad and couldn't imagine the pain she must be feeling. Jasmine had loved Mr. McClain very much also. She remembered how he and Summer's mom had always treated her like their other daughter. She couldn't help thinking back to when he, Mrs. McClain, and Summer had been there for her during one of her toughest times. Her mom had been working three jobs just to take care of her. She hated seeing her mother so tired. When she got home they barely exchanged words because Victoria would collapse across the bed and would be asleep instantly every day after working nearly eighteen hours. Jasmine couldn't bear to see her mother like that. She decided that she had to help her. She confided in Summer that she was going to drop out of school for one semester and get a job so that she could take some of the burden off her mother. She figured if she worked for one semester she could help her get back on her feet.

"What? Jasmine I don't think that's a very good idea. There has to be something else we can think of to help her besides you dropping out of school. And anyway, your mom wouldn't allow you to do that." They sat for hours brainstorming different ideas of how they could help but couldn't come up with anything that was reasonable. Finally, Summer had an idea.

"Jazz, let's talk to my parents and see if they can come up with something."

Jasmine was absolutely against it at first. Then she thought about it. "Do you really think they'll be able to come up with something? I mean, we've thought of a ton of things and none of them were good ideas."

"I'm sure my parents can think of something. Anyway, whatever they come up with it has to be better than you dropping out of school."

"Okay. We can talk to them but I don't know. I just know that I have to help her somehow."

"Well, it won't be by you dropping out of school."

After they spoke to David and Simone, they didn't think twice. When Victoria came to pick Jasmine up the next day from Summer's house, Simone asked her if she could come in. Jasmine remembered how considerate they had been of Victoria's feelings. Simone asked Summer and Jasmine to go to Summer's room, but Jasmine stood in the hallway upstairs listening.

"Victoria, Jasmine shared with us that you've been working a lot of hours and she's really concerned about you," Simone said.

"I have been working a lot. I have to in order to take care of Jasmine. I didn't realize she was so concerned though."

David chimed in, "We would like to help you. Please accept this gift from us." He extended his hand that held a check. Jasmine was so excited that they were going to help her mom. She wondered how much they were giving her.

Victoria looked down at the check David was holding. "I really appreciate that, but there's no way I could take that from you all."

Jasmine wanted to yell, "Mom, take the check! You know we need the money!" Her mom was used to doing everything on her own and her pride was clearly getting in the way. How could she turn down their gift when they needed the money so badly?

David and Simone were as persistent as she was. They wouldn't hear of her not accepting it. "Victoria, please take it. I have to tell you, Jasmine was contemplating quitting school and picking up a job in order to help you," Simone said.

"She will do no such thing." She paused. "Okay. I will take it but on one condition. You have to allow me to pay you back."

"That's fine, whenever you are able to. There's no rush," David said.

"Thank you," Victoria replied, humbly. She took the check. Jasmine was relieved that her mom finally gave in. She knew how stubborn Victoria could be. She never knew how much the check was for, but knew it had to have been a lot because it was enough for her mom to quit one of the jobs and cut her hours on the other part-time job.

David and Simone didn't let Victoria leave before they offered to have Jasmine come over to their home after school for dinner every day until her mom got home. Victoria accepted gracefully.

Jasmine recalled how thankful and relieved she had been that her mom was able to work less and that she didn't have to quit school. Summer and her family had been there for her and her mom when they needed them the most. They had been really good friends to them.

SNAPPING out of her daydream, Jasmine went back for another round of Oreos. This time, she finished the rest of the bag. Then she started on what was left of the family size bag of nacho cheese Doritos in the drawer that she had been eating earlier. She finished them off and tossed the empty bag on her night stand. She glanced over at the clock. It was 2:55 already.

"Aw man!" She hadn't realized how much time had passed since she hung up from Summer. She knew Summer would be there in a few minutes because she was never late. She jumped off the bed and dashed into the bathroom.

Her stomach was hurting something awful now. She felt miserable. *I've got to snap out of this before Summer gets here.* She held her stomach, hoping the cramps would go away. She looked at her reflection as she passed by the mirror. She hated how fat she looked. Everyone else thought her size eight frame was perfect but to her she looked hideous.

She made her way over to the toilet and stood over it with the lid lifted. *Why do I keep doing this to myself? If I could just lose enough weight, I'll stop.* She stuck her finger down her throat until everything she had just eaten came back up. She stood there a second and took a deep breath, relieved that she now felt better.

"Jasmine!" Summer was on time like clockwork.

"Shoot" she said under her breath, then yelled, "Hold on! I'm coming!"

She raced over to the sink and grabbed her wash cloth, wiping her clammy, sweaty face, and then brushed her teeth so there was no trace of vomit left on her breath. She looked at her reflection in the mirror. *There. That's much better. No one should think anything.*

Jasmine jogged down the hallway to her room but could see over the banister that Summer was standing by the door looking up at her.

"Girl, you can never be ready on time. You better come on before I change my mind."

"You better not change your mind. Give me two minutes. I'm ready. I just need to jump in my clothes."

Summer chuckled. "Then you're not ready, Jazz. Hurry up."

Jasmine ran into her room and quickly removed her gym shorts and old t-shirt. She stuffed herself into her favorite pair of partially faded jeans, grabbed a clean t-shirt, stuck her arms and head in the shirt, and then yelled, "Ready!" Not wanting to be scolded anymore by Summer, she grabbed her purse, put on her favorite lip gloss, and rushed downstairs.

Without looking back, Summer headed out the door.

Jasmine knew she was irritated. She didn't say a word. She just smiled and followed behind her.

She looked at her reflection as she passed by the mirror. She hated how fat she looked.

CHAPTER 12

Summer

I can't believe I let Jazz convince me to come here, Summer thought as she dragged herself into Di Maio's behind Jasmine.

"It's phat in here," Jasmine said excitedly.

"Jazz, it's too many people here. I'm really not up to this right now. I should have stayed home. Let's just leave," she said as she began stepping backwards toward the door.

Jasmine grabbed her arm and gave her a light tug. "Let's just stay for a little while," she said, whining. "All you were doing at home was sitting in your bedroom anyway and since you have to eat, you might as well eat your favorite pizza. *Right?*"

"I guess."

"Okay then. Let's go." Still holding Summer's arm, Jasmine pulled her in the direction of the first table she saw that was available.

Frustrated with Jasmine and herself for coming along, Summer hesitantly followed behind Jasmine with her shoulders slumped over and plopped down in a chair. *Why do I always let her talk me into stuff?*

Jasmine scanned the room. "There's Alexis and Brandon over there." She raised her hand and pointed in their direction, then waved at them when she saw them look her way.

"Umm hmmm," Summer responded, looking down at her menu. She and Jasmine never altered their order. It was always the same. Her mind drifted to her father. She thought about how much she missed him.

"And there's Macy, Raquel, and ughh Monique over there."

"Umm hmmm."

"What? Is that Brandon and that fine Dre over there with Monique and her crew? Shoot. They're both cute."

"Yeah." Summer's eyes never left the menu.

"There's Mickey and Minnie over there."

"Ummm hmmm."

"Summer!"

"Huh?" She looked up at Jasmine, wondering what her problem was.

"You're not even listening to me."

"Yeah, I hear you."

"Yeah, right," she said, sticking her lips out. "Anyway. Is Antoine going to meet us here?"

"No. I still couldn't reach him. It's not like him not to respond to my calls or to go this long without calling me."

"That's crazy. I wonder—"

"Hello, ladies." Jasmine was cut off by the curly-haired, dumpy waitress now standing at their table with an order tablet in her hand.

"Hi," they both responded.

"My name is Beth, and I'll be your waitress today. What can I get you ladies to drink?"

"I'll have pink lemonade," Jasmine spoke first.

"Okay. Got it. And for you?"

"I'll have the same thing."

"Gotcha. I'll go ahead and get those drinks for you and I'll be right back to take your order."

Before Beth could walk away, Summer said, "If it's okay with you, can we go ahead and order now? We already know what we want." She didn't want to prolong being there any longer than necessary.

"Sure. What can I get for you?"

"We want a medium deep dish pepperoni pizza."

"Got it. I'll put your order in right away and I'll be back with your drinks," she said as she jotted down their order and turned to walk away.

While they were waiting for their pizza, Jasmine continued making small talk about people that were there and about school starting in a month.

Summer thought, *Starting back to school in a month.* That was something else she wasn't looking forward to. Jasmine talked while Summer's mind was still miles away. The waitress slipped over to the table, sat their drinks down, and left without interrupting Jasmine's one way conversation. She was still talking a mile a minute when finally she was cut off by a girl from school who walked up to their table.

"Hi, Summer. Hi, Jazz."

Summer looked up. "Hey, Alexis."

"Hey, Alexis," Jasmine said.

Another girl from their school walked up right behind her. "Hey, Jazz and Summer."

"Hey, Erica." They both spoke in unison.

"Summer, I was really sorry to hear about your dad. I met him a few times. He was really nice," Alexis said.

Erica chimed in. "Yeah, me too. I'm really sorry about what happened."

"Thanks. I appreciate it."

Alexis changed the subject. "Are you all going to come back on Friday? They're having a special buffet with all you can eat pizza and other stuff. Everyone's talking about coming and then going bowling afterwards."

"No, I—"

"You know, we might just do that," Jasmine said, cutting Summer off.

Summer's eyes grew wide. She peered at Jasmine. *I told her I was only coming out today.*

Jasmine ignored her and looked the other way, continuing to talk to the girls. "That sounds like it'll be fun, especially since school will be starting soon."

"I know," Erica said, not too thrilled about going back to school.

The waitress came back. "I've got hot pizza for you ladies."

"I hope you all can make it. Hey, bring Antoine too. I'm surprised he's not hanging out with you all now. Anyway, we'll talk to you later," Alexis said.

"Bye," they all said together.

The waitress had barely put down the pizza, when Jasmine grabbed a slice and dug right in. "Ummm. This is good."

Summer took a slice and began eating. "Yeah it is good."

She reached for her glass of lemonade and took a large gulp to wash down her pizza. She looked up at Jasmine who had finally stopped talking since her mouth was full of pizza. Before Summer could finish her first slice she noticed that Jasmine was almost done devouring her second slice and was reaching for another one.

"Girl, are you starving?"

"No, I'm just hungry."

They continued eating in silence. Summer pushed herself to eat a third slice and was stuffed when she finished. Usually they would split what was left and take it home.

"Do you mind if I have some more?"

"No, go ahead." Summer wondered how Jasmine could eat another bite. She was surprised Jasmine hadn't gained any weight considering how her appetite seemed to have increased lately. In fact, Jasmine's usual size eight body was smaller than usual. She wasn't as small as Summer, but she was definitely smaller than usual. Where did she put it all? Jasmine finished off the rest of the pizza all by herself. Summer watched her in disbelief as she wiped the crumbs from her mouth.

Summer's attention was pulled away by the sound of the chair next to her scooting on the floor.

"Hey, I haven't seen you all here before." Summer looked up. Dre was sitting in the chair next to her. He was the new kid at school who transferred last year—who also happened to be the star player of the varsity basketball team. *Why would he want to talk to me and Jasmine? Not to mention just a few minutes ago he was talking to Monique, Raquel, and Macy. He's acting like he knows us.* Summer had seen him at school. She and Jasmine had admired his mad basketball skills from a distance. He was very popular among the girls but he'd never talked to them before. He moved his chair so close to Summer, he was in her personal space. The scent of his cologne filled the air and her nose. She scooted her chair away from him, hoping he realized how uncomfortable he was making her.

"We come here all the time, but I don't remember seeing you here before either," Jasmine responded.

He moved his chair closer to Summer. She looked at him oddly. He hadn't gotten the message.

Dre began whispering in Summer's ear. "So. What's your name?" She could feel his hot breath on her ear.

Obviously annoyed, she scooted her chair away, making a wider distance between them than she did before. With her eyes narrowed, she looked at him with a frown and responded, "Summer."

"You're really cute. Why do you have to look so mean?"

"I—"

"Oh, she's just having a bad day," Jasmine said. "She doesn't usually look that mean." Jasmine gave her a look that said, *Come on, Summer. He's cute! Get it together.*

Summer agreed mentally that he was cute but she wasn't in the mood for nonsense. Why did he have to sit so close? She figured that he was probably interested in either Macy, Raquel, or Monique since he was with them. If so, then why was he sitting in her face?

"Oh, okay. Well, my name is Dre. You might remember me from the basketball team at school. I transferred in last year. I'm the highest scorer on the team." Dre smiled and leaned back in his chair. "Can I call you some time?"

"Nah. I really don't give my number out like that, but I'm sure I'll see you around."

Jasmine looked at Summer in disbelief with her mouth hanging open. Dre looked equally shocked.

By his reaction, Summer figured that he wasn't used to being turned down. She chuckled to herself. *Am I supposed to care that he's the star basketball player and fall all over him like all those desperate girls do?*

Summer looked over at the group of friends that he was standing with earlier. Raquel and Macy appeared to be in a deep conversation with the other guy. Monique was looking at her curiously.

"Dang, girl! You are cold," Dre said.

She turned her attention back to him. She looked at him with a straight face and said, "Not really," then turned to Jasmine and said, "Jazz. Are you ready to go?"

"No. Not really we just got here. Why—"

"Dre!" Monique was now yelling at him from across the room. She was signaling to him to come over to where she was, but to no avail. He wasn't paying her the least bit of attention.

"It looks like Monique is trying to get your attention," Summer said.

"Aww, she'll be alright." He kept his eyes on Summer. "So, when will you be here again? Since I can't get your number, maybe we can hang out before school starts back. Maybe I can hit you up on Facebook."

"Naw."

"Is that your girl?" Jasmine interrupted.

"We're just cool."

Monique was now standing at their table, leaning over Summer. "Dre. What are you doing? We're getting ready to leave. I thought you were hanging out with us."

Dre never looked at her. He kept his eyes on Summer. "I am. I'm just talking to my new friends for a few minutes. I'll be back over there."

New friends? Monique looked at Jasmine, trying to figure out what was really going on.

"Alright. Well, you need to hurry up," Monique said with an attitude, and then turned to walk away. As she turned, she swung her arm, hitting Summer's glass of lemonade. It fell and spilled all over Summer. Her shirt and jeans were drenched.

Summer shot up from her chair. "Ahhhh!" She stood, paralyzed by the after effect of the cold ice and lemonade that was now all over her.

"Oh, I am so sorry," Monique said, her voice dripping with sarcasm.

Summer was finally able to move enough to grab the napkins on the table and attempted to dry herself off. Everyone in the restaurant was looking at them, observing what had happened. The waitress ran over holding towels to assist Summer in her effort to wipe up the lemonade. She handed the towels to Summer.

"Thank you." While she was still wiping herself off, Summer looked at Monique. She had a smug smile plastered on her face. *What is she smiling about? Does she think this is funny?* She couldn't believe this was happening. She looked at Jasmine who was staring Monique down.

In an instant, Monique's smile was gone. She turned her attention back to Dre. In a very flat voice Monique said, "Come on, Dre." She gave Summer a stone cold, evil look, then turned and walked away.

"What was up with that?" Jasmine said, obviously irritated.

"I don't know what's up with her. Anyway, here's a few more napkins," Dre said, then handed them to Summer. She snatched them from him and made a final attempt to sop up the rest of the sticky lemonade.

She reached in her purse and handed a ten dollar bill across the table to Jasmine. "Jazz, I'm going to get the car. Come on out."

"Okay. I'm going to run to the restroom and I'll be right out."

"I guess. Please hurry," Summer responded, not caring how frustrated she sounded.

"Hey, you sure I can't call you?" Dre asked.

Summer looked at him with a straight face that was even colder than the lemonade that was now sticky and drying on her clothes. She turned and walked away.

"I guess not."

She walked out the door shaking her head. *This guy is unbelievable. Why did I even come here?*

CHAPTER 13

Simone

Simone was lying in her bed. It had been over a month since David had been gone. Scanning her eyes around the room, she realized she was tired of being between those four walls. She sat up and threw her legs over the side of the bed. She looked over at her dresser mirror and gawked at her reflection. It was hard to believe that she was the same woman that was usually so well-groomed and put together. Her hair was wild and all over her head. The only reason she had been able to muster up the energy to take a shower and brush her teeth had been because she didn't want to offend Big Momma or Summer when she sat down to eat.

The phone is ringing. AGAIN. Why don't they just leave me alone? She looked at the caller ID. *Chicago Police Department.* It was on its third ring. Summer was still gone with Jasmine. Simone knew Big Momma wasn't going to answer it since she asked her not to. She was tired of hearing the phone ringing. She was also tired of avoiding Sergeant Tooley. On the fourth ring, Simone reached over and grabbed the receiver.

"Hello." The pit of her stomach formed a tight ball. She still wasn't ready to face talking about David's murder.

"Hello. May I speak with Mrs. McClain?"

"This is."

"Hi, ma'am. This is Sergeant Tooley. I'm sorry for bothering you. I know you and your family's going through a very tough time. I'm certainly not going to take very much of your time, but I have a few questions that I need to ask you so that we can move forward in our investigation. Can I have just a moment of your time?"

"Sure," she said hesitantly. She knew she had to face him at some time.

"Okay great. Thank you. First, I'd like to know if you heard Officer McClain talk at any time about any disagreements or confrontations he may have had with anyone prior to the incident."

"No. Nothing at all."

"Do you know of anyone that didn't like him?"

"No one. David didn't have any enemies that I know of. Just out of curiosity, why are you asking about people he knew? He was at work in an area where there's always crime. Isn't it obvious that it was someone he didn't know?"

"We're just trying to look at every possible scenario. We're being very careful not to miss anything."

"Hmmm. I see."

"One more question. Before the incident, had he mentioned any altercations or encounters on or off the job with anyone that may have escalated beyond normal?"

Wasn't that the same question he asked before but phrased differently? And why does he keep referring to David's murder as 'the incident'? She took a deep breath. *I'm not going to let this irritate me. Perhaps he's considering my feelings and thinks that choice of words will make me feel more comfortable.* Simone relaxed her shoulders.

"I'm sorry, Sergeant Tooley. David hadn't mentioned anything like that. Every day was pretty much the same from what he'd told me. Have you tried talking to his partner, Jay? If David wasn't at home with us, he was usually with him."

"Well, we have but…" He paused. "Well, he's been somewhat unavailable. The last time I spoke with him, which was earlier in the investigation, he was still pretty upset but, from what I could gather from him, he said pretty much the same thing you did. Nothing was different."

Unavailable? "I see."

"Well, Mrs. McClain, that pretty much answers the questions I have for now. We will try to bother you as little as possible from here on out, but I may have to call you from time to time as new information develops. Although many of the details that we find will be confidential until a suspect or suspects are arrested, we definitely want to keep you informed of how the investigation is going. We want to get that scum off the streets."

"Thank you very much, Sergeant Tooley." She was actually glad now that she'd finally spoken to him. She actually felt a sense of relief.

"You're welcome, ma'am. Have a good day."

"Thanks. Goodbye."

"Goodbye."

Simone hung up the phone, walked into her bathroom, and took a long, hot bubble bath. She washed her hair and put on some clothes. An hour later, she sat in the family room with Big Momma.

"Are you hungry, baby?" Big Momma asked.

"Not right now, but I could probably eat later."

"Okay. Well, dinner is ready whenever you are. You have to eat to keep up your strength."

"Okay." She smiled. "I spoke with Sergeant Tooley today."

"Oh really?"

"Yes, I finally answered when he called the last time."

"I'm glad you did. You know I would have screened the calls for as long as you would have wanted me to, but it was best that you went on and talked to him."

"You're right, and I do feel better now that I did."

The front door opened and Summer walked in. "Hi."

"Hi, baby." Big Momma looked at her strangely.

"Hi, honey," Simone said, glancing at Summer. She did a double take, realizing Summer's appearance wasn't right. She looked at her closer then frowned. "What in the world happened to your clothes? You look a mess."

"Oh. Jazz convinced me to go to Di Maio's and someone accidentally knocked over a glass of lemonade on me."

"Oh. Well, you need to go and get out of those nasty clothes and clean yourself up."

"Yes, ma'am." Summer headed straight to the bathroom and Big Momma went back to her conversation with Simone.

"So, how did things go with Sergeant Tooley? What did he want?"

"It went pretty well. It turns out that he only wanted to ask a few questions in order to rule out anyone that David might have known as a suspect."

"Oh. I'd be really surprised if it was anyone David knew. He's never had any enemies. Not even when he was a kid. People always liked him."

"I know. That's what I told him, but you know, I guess they have to consider everything and everybody."

"Right. I can understand that. They don't need to leave no rock unturned. That heathen or heathens need to be caught." Simone could see the pain on Big Momma's face.

"You know what?" Simone paused. "Sergeant Tooley said something else while I was talking to him that really concerned me."

"What was that, baby?"

"When I asked him if he had talked to Jay, he hesitated, and then he said that Jay was unavailable."

"Unavailable? What does that mean?"

"He didn't elaborate but that concerned me. He did mention that Jay was really upset and they got what information they could from him."

"Well, he's obviously upset just like the rest of us. They were as close as any set of friends could be."

"Exactly. I'm going to give him a call. I don't want to keep worrying about him." She reached over, grabbed the phone, and dialed Jay's number.

"Hello?"

Simone was surprised not to hear Jay's voice on the other end of the line. Instead, it was Zoe's sweet, mellow voice that rang through the receiver.

"Oh, Zoe, how are you?"

"Simone. I've been doing pretty good. How are you doing?"

"Oh, we're making it one day at a time. Thanks for asking. It's been so busy around here after David's—after the service, I hadn't gotten a chance to thank you for the beautiful painting you made us."

"Oh, it was my pleasure. I actually found it to be therapeutic for myself. You know how much we loved David. He was a brother to Jay and me."

"David loved you all too. We all do. Zoe, I have to ask you, with all of that talent, when are you going to get yourself enrolled in art school? I know you've wanted to do that for a long time."

"Yes, I have but—"

"But what? What's keeping you from doing it?"

"Something always seems to come up when I think about enrolling. I will someday."

"Only put off until tomorrow what you are willing to die having left undone. Do you know who said that?"

"No, I can't say I do."

"Picasso."

"Really? Wow. That's something to really think about. Thanks, Simone. David always used to push me to go to school too. You sound just like him." She laughed. "I appreciate your concern."

"You can't sleep on your dreams, baby girl."

Zoe chuckled. "I'm glad you called. I've been thinking about you guys a lot. I just wanted to give you all a little time before trying to call or come by."

"Oh, sweetie. I appreciate that. We're still taking one day at a time but you can call any time."

"You know I'm here for you all. Jay and I both are."

"Thank you so much. It means a lot. Speaking of Jay, how is he doing?"

"Not so good. You know, with the loss of David and all, he just hasn't been himself. He's not taking it well at all. He's been so mean and irritable and has isolated himself from everyone. That's actually why I'm here and have been answering his calls. He really hasn't wanted to talk to anyone."

"Well, I was going to ask to speak to him but if he's not wanting to talk, I really understand. I've been feeling the same way. Just let him know that we love him and that I asked about him."

"Hold on a minute. I'm sure he'll want to speak to you."

"Okay."

"Jay? It's Simone. She wants to speak to you," Zoe called out. A few moments later he came to the phone.

"Hey, Simone. How are you?" His voice somewhat groggy.

"Hi, Jay. I'm doing pretty good, considering. How are you doing?"

"Oh, I'm doing okay."

"Are you sure about that?"

"Well—"

"Jay. In spite of all that I'm going through, I know this is tough for you as well. If something is going on with you, don't feel like you have to keep it from me because you're worried about me. I'm here for you now, and I always will be. I can tell that something is wrong. By you not telling me what it is, it will only make me worry about you."

He took a deep breath. "Okay, Simone. You've never made it easy to get anything past you." He chuckled.

"That's right. So what's going on?"

"Well, of course you know I'm having a hard time dealing with David's death. That's obvious."

"Right."

"I probably should have taken some time off work like my lieutenant suggested but I didn't. I went back anyway but I couldn't concentrate on anything except finding the scum that killed David. They became concerned that my interference would hinder the investigation because I wasn't exactly following protocol. They also said they were concerned for my well-being. I've been forced to take a leave of absence, with pay of course, and have been ordered to attend grief counseling. So there you have it. That's what's going on with me."

"Oh, Jay. I'm so sorry. You know, sometimes things seem really bad when it happens, but it works out to be for the best. I believe they're really looking out for you. It may be good for you to be off right now. I'm sure you'll be back sooner than you think."

"You know, Simone, the more time I have to think, the more I'm not so sure I want to go back. It'll never be the same there again without David."

"But, Jay, you love your job. I know right now it's tough learning to work without David, but I'm sure you'll change your mind after some time off. Counseling will help also."

"Yeah, maybe. The part that really made me mad was them not wanting me to work on David's case. He was my partner." He sniffled. "What a slap in the face. I tell you what though, I'm going to find who killed him, whether I'm on the force or not, if it's the last thing I do. I promise you that, Simone."

"Jay, please be careful. I know you loved David, but let them have a chance to find out who did it. Please, Jay. Don't jeopardize yourself or the case. You won't be able to forgive yourself if you did that."

"Okay, Simone."

"You promise?" She knew he was stubborn as a bull and would tell her anything to shut her up.

"I promise."

"You let me know if there is anything I can do for you."

"Okay. I appreciate it."

"I mean it, Jay."

He laughed between sniffles. "I know you do."

"Okay. I'll talk to you later."

"I love you, and you take care of yourself."

"I love you too. Talk to you later."

"Bye."

Big Momma looked up from her puzzle. "It sounds like Jay is having a tough time."

"He definitely is. We have to keep him in our prayers." Simone felt her stomach growl. She stood up and headed to the kitchen. Big Momma followed behind her.

CHAPTER 14

Summer

A COUPLE OF weekends had passed since the fiasco at Di Maio's. Jasmine had tried daily since then to get Summer to go to different places but she refused. She knew Jasmine was just trying to cheer her up by getting her out of the house. Her response was always the same. "Jazz, I'm just going to stay around the house for a while." Inside Summer appreciated what her friend was trying to do but she was determined that this time she was going to stick to her decision to lay low until school started. It had just been overwhelming being around so many people. Being around them made her realize how broken she still felt inside. Her mind had been turning constantly like a whirlwind with confusing thoughts and questions about her father's death. She was overwhelmed with all the questions. *Why did God let Daddy die? Why did he have to die at the hands of an evil murderer when he was the best person in the world? I know I'm not perfect but why do I have to live the rest of my life without a father when I've tried to do things the right way?* Summer was beginning to feel bitterness growing in her that she'd never experienced before. She forced her mind to go elsewhere. She figured staying to herself was the best thing to do.

After Summer wouldn't change her mind, Jasmine went back to Di Maio's alone a few times but made sure to report back all the latest gossip.

"Girl, check this out. The word is Monique and that guy Dre are not dating but they have been hanging out. Whatever that means."

"So why was she looking at me all crazy?" Summer asked.

"Well, from what I hear she really likes him. A lot more than he likes her."

"That was obvious the way he was all up in my face."

Jasmine laughed. "You weren't paying him any attention. And it was so obvious that he was getting on your nerves."

"He really was. All up in my face. Breathing on my neck. Uhhhh! She can have that buster. No interference from me. I don't care if he is a *star* basketball player."

Jasmine laughed again. "Dre was right. You are cold."

"I don't have time for no drama. Then I had to deal with my mother asking why I looked a mess when I got home. All I need is for her to be worrying about me when she already has a lot on her mind with Daddy's…Like I said, I just don't need any drama."

"I know. What did you tell your mom?"

"I just told her someone accidentally knocked some lemonade on me. I guess it was an accident. That look Monique had on her face had me wondering."

"I know! I caught that too," Jasmine said.

"You know her better than I do. Do you think she did it on purpose? I mean, I don't know why. I'm not even thinking about him."

"When we were friends I never saw her trip over a dude but she is deceitful so I don't know. I wouldn't put it past her. She does like him. That I do know."

"Well, whatever. She should have seen that I wasn't thinking about him with his arrogant self." She rolled her eyes thinking about how obnoxious Dre was. As far as Monique, she figured that if she had been trying to be funny it would blow over in the next few weeks before school started.

SUMMER spent the last couple of weeks mostly to herself listening to her iPod and reading. She finally got tired of sitting in the house.

"Mom, I still need to get a few more school supplies before school starts."

"Honey, are you sure you're ready to go back to school next week? I mean, it's so soon."

"I'm ready. I'm kind of tired of sitting in the house anyway." She looked at the concerned look on Simone's face. "Really, Mom. I'm going to be fine. I want to go back next week."

"Okay." Simone didn't sound convinced. "If you think you're ready. If you change your mind, it's okay. I want you to be okay with going back. A lot has changed for you."

You can say that again, Summer thought. *Things will never be the same without Daddy.* Summer knew her mother was right but felt she was also being too overly protective. She had told her many times over the past weeks, "Mom, I'm really okay. I just haven't felt like being around a lot of people yet." Now that some time had passed she thought that going back to school might help get her father's death off her mind.

THE evening before the first day of school had finally come. Summer had been calling Antoine all summer and still hadn't been able to reach him. She was pretty anxious to see him at school the next day. She really had a bone to pick with him but in case something was wrong she'd decided she'd give him a chance to explain why he'd just vanished. She was really worried about him. This was not like him at all to just disappear and not talk to her for weeks at a time.

Summer forced her mind to go elsewhere. She was ready to call it a night. She got up from her chair and began looking at her clothes that she'd laid out for school the next day. She hadn't felt like putting together anything real special. She lifted her Button-Up lavender and white striped shirt and made sure it was still neat from where she ironed it earlier. Then she checked her crisp ironed jeans for any wrinkles she might have missed. Everything looked good. She walked back to her bed and lay down.

I'll see how things go tomorrow, Summer thought. Her mind went back to her father which made her sad. *It definitely won't be the same not having Daddy here to send me off to school on the first day like he always did.* She smiled thinking of their yearly ritual. He'd come to her room and wake her up bright and early with his cheerful voice, acting like it was her first day ever going to school. "Rise and shine, pumpkin." He had done that every year since she started pre-school. She knew she would have to get through it without him.

CHAPTER 15

Summer

THE SUN PEEKED through Summer's pink curtains and cast light on her sleeping face. Frowning, she turned over and pulled the sheet over her head. Then there was a knock on the door followed by her mom's voice. "Summer, sweetie. It's time to get up for school." Her alarm clock hadn't gone off yet. She wished her mom had waited just a few more minutes.

In a groggy voice, Summer responded, "Okay, Mom." She felt tired and didn't feel like getting up but knew she didn't want to stay in the house another day.

"Baby, are you *sure* you want to go to school today?"

"Yes, Mom. I'm going to be okay. I promise. I'll be fine."

"Okay, well it's time to get up. Big Momma's getting ready to cook breakfast for you. Hurry up so you'll have time to eat."

"Yes, ma'am." As soon as Summer heard the door close, she took her pillow and put it over her head hoping to steal just a few more minutes of sleep. The alarm went off.

"Ahhhh!" Without removing the pillow from her head Summer reached out and slammed the snooze button on her alarm clock. *Just a few more minutes. Just a few minutes more.* Her stomach growled. The smell of bacon invaded the space around her and filled her nose with the savory scent. There was no way she was going to sleep now with that distraction. She threw the pillow off her head onto her bed, and then peeked through squinted eyes at her alarm clock. The display read 5:30 a.m. *I might as well get up. I'm obviously not going to get any more sleep.* She sat up and stretched her arms far above her head. She threw her feet over the side of the bed, stepped into her pink fluffy house shoes, and walked to the bathroom.

Forty-five minutes later, Summer was dressed and ready for school, sitting at the table with Big Momma and her mom. She rushed her breakfast down so she wouldn't be late.

"Slow down. You have a few minutes before you have to leave," Big Momma said.

"I have to hurry, Big Momma. I told Jazz I would pick her up."

"Well, you make sure you aren't rushing when you get behind the wheel. You have to drive safely, Okay?" Simone insisted.

"I am, Mom. That's why I'm trying to hurry." She stood up holding her last piece of bacon in one hand and grabbed her backpack from the floor with her other hand and threw it over her shoulder. She guzzled the last of her orange juice down and set the glass back on the table.

"I love you." She planted a kiss on Simone's cheek.

"I love you too, Sweetie."

"I love you too, Big Momma," she said to her grandmother after kissing her on the cheek.

"I love you too, baby. Have a good day."

"Thanks. Bye," Summer said, chewing her bacon as she headed out the door.

SUMMER pulled into a parking space of the student parking lot. She looked at the clock on her dashboard. It read 7:20 a.m. *Whew. Ten minutes to spare.* She looked over at Jasmine who was trying to stuff what was left of a Honey Bun into her mouth.

"Come on, Jazz. We gotta go before we're late."

"Okay. Let me eat the rest of this. We have a few minutes."

"Girl, come on." Summer frowned. She felt disgusted with how Jasmine was gorging herself with food lately. "How can you eat like that anyway? That is your fifth Honey Bun."

"Fourth," Jasmine said with a full mouth as she stuffed the last bite in.

Summer shook her head and opened the car door. "Let's go," she said as she stepped out of the car and closed the door behind her. She took off walking at a fast pace.

Jasmine jumped out of the car. "Hold up!" She caught up with Summer. Licking the frosting off her lips, she said, "Did you hear the commercial on the radio this morning about the concert this weekend? Trey Songz is coming here, to Chicago."

"Really? No, I hadn't heard about it but that would be cool. Do you want to go?"

"Oh, yeah. All I need is my outfit and I'm in."

"I already know what I want to wear. Yeah, let's go for sure," Summer said as she swung open the door to the school and walked into the hallway.

"What are you going to wear?"

"I'll tell you later. Gotta go," Summer said, as she headed toward her locker.

"Summer, slow down! I'm still talking to you. Tell me now. Your locker is right by mine."

"I know," Summer said, pulling open the door to her locker. "But I don't have time. Go to class. I'll talk to you later."

Jasmine rolled her eyes and shoved her backpack in her locker. "I am going to class but I have to go to the bathroom first. I'll see you later." Jasmine left going toward the bathroom.

"Hey, Summer," Latoya said.

"What's up, Summer," Brandon said.

Man, I'm never going to get to class. "Hey, Latoya. Hey, Brandon."

"I didn't get a chance to talk to you at your father's funeral, but I wanted to tell you that I'm sorry to hear about what happened," Latoya said.

"Yeah, me too. I can't even imagine losing my pops," Brandon said.

Summer lowered her voice. "Thank you."

"Oh! I'm sorry. I didn't mean to make you feel bad," Latoya said.

"It's okay. It's just still kinda hard to get used to, but I appreciate that you all came to the funeral. That meant a lot seeing everyone there."

"You know it," Brandon said.

Summer looked at her watch. She only had one minute before the bell rang. "Well, I've got to get to class. I'll talk to you all later."

"Yeah, see ya later," Latoya said.

Summer jogged down the hall to her class.

Summer looked at the clock wishing class was over. Although she was there physically, the entire time she sat in class her mind was elsewhere. Finally, it was over. She darted out the door.

One more class. Summer stood at her locker trying to find her English book. The day was almost over. It had gone pretty well in spite of everyone telling her how sorry they were about her dad passing. Although she appreciated their kind thoughts, she hoped they wouldn't keep talking about him and what happened. Constantly hearing about it seemed to stir up the bitterness she'd been feeling and made her think about the fact that his killer was still running free.

"Hey, Summer," Jasmine said, walking up to her locker.

"Hey. Jazz. Are you riding home with me?"

"No, I have to stay after so I can talk to my counselor. I'll call you later, though."

"Okay. That's cool."

"Did you see Antoine today?" Jasmine said as she searched for something in her purse.

"No, I haven't seen him today." *I may have to go by his house.* "This is crazy. Antoine has never missed school. Well, not since my dad got him to quit hanging with the wrong crowd," she said while still shuffling through her books and papers. "I cannot find my English book." While she was pushing books to the side, some of her notebooks and papers fell out of her locker.

"Summer, why are you so messy? School just started," Jasmine said, stooping down to help her pick them up.

Summer laughed. "You've got your nerve. Let me look at your locker. If it's not messy now, I'll give you a day or two." They both laughed because they knew Jasmine was definitely the messier of the two of them. Summer stood up with her arms full of papers and notebooks. Someone bumped into her elbow.

"Why don't you watch what you're doing?" She turned around to find Monique facing her.

"Oh, I'm sorry, Monique. I didn't see you standing there."

Summer looked behind Monique and noticed that her friends, Macy and Raquel, were standing close behind with mischievous grins on their faces.

Monique turned and looked at her friends. "How did she not see me and I'm standing right here next to her?" She turned back to Summer and looked her up and down. "I think you did it on purpose with your stuck-up self."

Summer looked at her with a frown, and then looked at Jasmine. *I guess this silly girl is still tripping about that dude.*

"Monique, what's wrong with you? She said she was sorry. What's up with you?" Jasmine interrupted.

"Jazz, you're not in this. This is between me and the rich girl."

"I am in it because she's my best friend. She accidentally bumped you and she said she was sorry. You're sounding a whole lot like a hater to me. You need to let it go."

"Hater? Whatever, Jazz." She threw her hand in the air towards Jasmine. "Like I said Jazz, this has nothing to do with you. Your little friend just better stay out of my way. I don't like her anyway."

"You don't like her? Why? Because of that weak dude Dre? You need to stop acting so silly," Jasmine said, in a louder voice, stepping toward Monique.

"It don't have nothin' to do with Dre. I don't appreciate her hitting me. I know she did it on purpose."

"Girl, you are still just as silly as you used to be. I'm still asking myself how I was ever friends with your silly behind. You need to grow up. She didn't hit you. She bumped into you. Or did you bump into her just to start some drama?" Jasmine said.

Summer didn't want Jasmine to get into any trouble over her. Speaking as calm as she could, she interjected, "Jazz, don't worry about it. Go on to class. I'm getting ready to go." As hard as it was to ignore Monique, Summer decided it would be best if she just walked away. Her face was burning hot and she could feel her blood boiling but she knew Monique wasn't worth it.

"Oh, you're ignoring me, Little Miss Stuck-up?" Monique let out a little chuckle.

Summer reached in her locker and put her papers and notebook inside. *There it is,* she thought. She reached for her English book.

"If you ever put your hands on me again you'll be sorry. You think you're so cute. I ought to slap you right now."

Without realizing it, Summer clenched her teeth together.

"Monique, you don't want to do that." She slammed the locker door while staring Monique in her eyes. She turned and walked away heading toward her class. She heard Jasmine still talking to her.

"Monique, you better back off. I'm not telling you again."

"Whatever, Jazz," Monique responded. Macy and Raquel laughed. Summer stopped at the door of her English class and looked down the hall. She saw that they were walking down the hall in the opposite direction. Jasmine took her jacket and math book out of her locker and closed it, then turned and headed toward the restroom.

Summer turned and walked briskly into the classroom and slid into her seat just before the late bell rang. Her head was pounding. Rubbing her head, she became even more frustrated that she was almost late because of mere nonsense. She couldn't concentrate on what Ms. Gonzales was saying because she was still thinking about what had just happened with Monique. She began chewing the end of her pencil. She wondered why she had to keep dealing with that ignorant girl.

"Summer? Summer? Summer!" Ms. Gonzales yelled.

"Ummm, Ummm, yes ma'am?"

"Well, we're waiting. Class is only an hour."

"Ummm, I'm sorry. I didn't hear what you asked. Can you repeat it?" Summer replied.

"I asked you to read the next section. Are you with us today, Summer? I mean, I know you're here but your mind seems to be elsewhere. Would you please read?"

She couldn't wait for school to be over so she could just get out of there. She was more removed at this point than she had been all day. She felt like she was having what felt like an out-of-body experience. She was so angry. First, images of people that could be her dad's murderer kept invading her thoughts, now Monique. She couldn't concentrate on the class. *I have to shake this off. I can't let her get in my head like this.*

"Summer, we're still waiting." Mrs. Gonzales was clearly losing her patience.

She finished reading the passage that Mrs. Gonzales asked her to read.

"Do you have any thoughts on that passage that you'd like to add, Summer?"

"No, ma'am,"

"Thank you, Summer. Class, you all are to read the next two chapters and—" Mrs. Gonzales was interrupted by the class bell ringing. It was the end of the day. Everyone jumped up and ran toward the door.

Whew, thank God this day is over and I can leave this class and this school for at least the rest of today.

Mrs. Gonzales yelled as everyone rushed for the door, "Class, your assignment is to complete this reading and answer the rest of the questions at the end."

Summer continued out the door with the other students. She could hear Mrs. Gonzales's voice still yelling, but fading away. "Have a good evening."

Summer had already packed her backpack before English with all of her other class homework assignments. She was relieved she didn't have to go back to her locker and chance another altercation with Monique. She wanted to talk to Jasmine, but she'd have to call her when she got home. While everyone else was in the school gathering at their lockers and in the hallway laughing and talking about what they were going to do after school, Summer took the opportunity to slide out the side door right to the student parking lot. For a brief second, she closed her eyes and took a deep breath as the fresh air swept across her face. She felt free.

The rest of the week has got to be better. It has to.

"Thank God this day is almost over," Summer said, relieved she hadn't had another ugly encounter with Monique like the one she'd had the day before.

"I know. I'm ready for the weekend but right now I'm getting ready to go to the bathroom." Jasmine reached in her locker and took out a bag of chili cheese Frito Lays.

"Jazz, you just went to the bathroom before lunch. And you're getting ready to eat again? You ate like a pig at—"

"You think you're cute, don't you, rich girl?" Monique said, cutting Summer off as she walked up to her and stood so close that Summer could feel her breath on her face.

"No, you do. Why are you all in her face?" Jasmine interjected.

"You're not that cute." Monique pushed Summer's shoulder and knocked her against the locker.

Jasmine stepped away from her locker and moved between Summer and Monique. She was standing even closer to Monique's face than Monique was to Summer's just seconds before. She stared Monique directly in her eyes and didn't flinch. "Push me."

"Come on, Jazz. I'm not thinking about her. Let's go," Summer said, tugging Jasmine's arm. Although Jasmine stumbled she held her footing and continued staring Monique down with a stone cold face that meant nothing but business.

"Naw. I want her to push me. She's just mad because that weak dude Dre doesn't want her," Jasmine yelled.

Monique looked at Jasmine with a smirk and walked around

her. "Whatever," she said and threw her hand in the air as she bumped into Summer and pushed past her.

Jasmine reached her hand out and pushed Monique so hard in the back of her head that she stumbled down the hallway. Startled, Monique caught her balance but couldn't keep a grip on her books and an orange drink that fell from her hand onto the floor. She turned around abruptly. Before Monique could say anything, Jasmine had run up to her and was standing right in her face again.

"What?" Jasmine said, staring her directly in her eyes.

Monique looked at her but didn't utter a word.

"What's going on down there, ladies?" Mr. Benson said as he walked down the hallway toward them.

"Nothing, Mr. Benson. We were just going to class," Summer responded quickly. "Come on, Jazz," she whispered.

Jasmine kept her eyes focused on Monique. Her look told Monique that she didn't care who was standing there. She was ready to beat her down.

"Well alright. Let's get moving people," Mr. Benson insisted with his puny voice, while he watched the girls through the tiny pair of glasses sitting at the tip of his nose.

Summer grabbed Jasmine's arm again and pulled her down the hall.

"It ain't over, rich girl," Monique said, holding the back of her head as she picked up her dripping, orange drink stained books from the floor.

"It sho ain't!" Jasmine shouted.

CHAPTER 16

Summer

THE WEEK WAS finally over and things had only gotten worse with Monique. If she wasn't walking past Summer making snide remarks, she was giving her evil looks or *accidentally* bumping into her in the hallway and knocking Summer's books out of her hands.

She was relieved she wouldn't have to go back to school for a couple of days. All the pressure was beginning to put a damper on her already broken spirit. She couldn't wait to get to her black Honda Accord that was parked right beside the gate where she always parked for a quick exit. She jumped in, turned on the ignition, put the car in the drive position, and pressed down on the gas. She headed straight for the highway. With the window down and her long black hair blowing in the wind, she began to think about everything that had happened in the past couple of months. She was feeling extremely overwhelmed. She turned on the radio since music always made her feel better. Instead of music, her favorite radio show was on. She turned up the volume. Jazz told her they'd been advertising the Trey Songz concert they were going to. Sassy Sasha's voice rang loudly through the speakers.

"Hey everybody out there. I've got two tickets to Trey Songz, the hottest concert of the year for the first caller who can name the title of the two songs I'm going to play next. The winner will win this hour's prize pack which includes two front row seats to the concert and backstage passes. You must listen closely and you must name each song correctly in order to win. This is the one and only Sassssssy Sasha on WHOT! HOTTTTT! 104.5FM. Your place for hot topics and the latest music. All day. Every day. After you've heard the entire song, call 312-392-WHOT. Again, the number to call is 312-392-WHOT.

As Summer drove, she listened and sang along with each song that followed while waiting for the contest lyrics. For a short time she thought she might be able to forget about all the things that weren't going well in her life. The same lyrics that usually uplifted her were now making her think of everything that was wrong. She began silently talking to God.

God, how could my life go from everything being perfect to total chaos? How does that happen? Why did you have to take my daddy away from me? Why won't you answer that question for me? I feel so bad about this but I'm mad at you for taking him. And why is all of this mess happening with Monique? I've never done anything to her and I don't deserve this.

For the first time since her dad died she was able to really express how she felt to God. She continued letting her emotions flow.

And why is it that when all of this mess is going on, one of my best friends disappears? Antoine didn't show up for school at all this week. It's been a whole month since I've seen or heard from him. I don't know if I could take it if something has happened to him too, God. Would you really let something happen to him after he started doing so good, God? Tears were pouring from her eyes. *God, how could you do this to me, again? I'm begging you. Please don't let anything happen to him too.*

She hoped after talking to God she'd feel better but she didn't. She was still angry and bitter. Some of her anger was directed toward Antoine. She was tired of calling him and decided to go to his apartment. Immediately, she could hear her mother's voice.

Summer. I don't want you going to Antoine's apartment. It's too dangerous over there. He's welcome to come here anytime, but you stay away from there. She tried to shake her mother's voice from her mind. At that moment she needed to know he was okay.

She wiped her tears with the back of her hand. *I know I told Mom I wouldn't go over there but I have to see if Antoine is okay. I won't stay long.* She took the next exit off the highway and detoured back toward Antoine's apartment.

Fifteen minutes later, she pulled into a parking space in front of Antoine's apartment. She sat there for a moment looking around and observing her surroundings before getting out. There were a group of guys standing about five apartments down from Antoine's place. Further down the street, there were a few more groups of guys and some girls hanging out. Her stomach began to feel uneasy and her shoulders were tense. *I'll walk up there really fast and I'll come right back if I don't get an answer after a minute.*

She opened the door to her car and stepped out real fast, kicking a bottle as her feet hit the ground. She slammed the door and clicked the lock button on her key fob. Holding her purse close to her side, she stepped over all the rubbish around her feet and began walking briskly toward his apartment.

Her father's voice came to her: *Summer, that area is very unsafe. I want you to stay away from there, baby.* She was beginning to feel like this was a bad idea, but it was too late to turn back now. Usually she loved when she heard her daddy's voice because she feared that one day she'd forget it. But right now wasn't the time. She shook his voice from her head and kept walking at a brisk pace. When she got to the stairs, she jogged up as quickly as she could.

She looked at the three doors on each side of her and then the one in the middle. *24A. That's the one.* She knocked on the door, then stood with her back to the door looking toward the street so she could see if someone walked up to her. There was no response at the door. She knocked again.

"Hey, Shawty!" She heard someone yell from down the street.

Oh my gosh! She looked in the direction where she heard the voice and saw a short, skinny guy waving his hand motioning for her to come to him. *Ooohh, what should I do? Why didn't I listen to what Mom and Daddy told me?* She was terrified. She looked at Antoine's door. It was still closed.

I better get to the car before this guy decides to come down here. She began walking toward the steps. Before she could step down the first one, she heard the door behind her open.

"Yes?" a raspy woman's voice spoke.

That doesn't sound like Antoine's mother. Summer stood at the step and turned back around.

A woman wearing a dingy white t-shirt, cut-off denim shorts, and dirty house shoes with holes in them stood in the doorway. She held a cigarette in her hand. A little boy of about five was standing beside her, holding onto one of her legs. He was eating a cracker. On the other side of her stood a little girl who looked to be about two. Summer was confused. *I know this is Antoine's apartment. Who is this lady?* She knew she had the right place. She'd been there before with her father to pick up Antoine. That was the first time he'd told her that he didn't want her going over there alone.

"Umm. I was looking for my friend." She paused. "Antoine."

The woman squinted her eyes and stared at Summer, then took a long draw from her cigarette. Then she scratched her head that was wrapped with a red and white scarf with pink sponge rollers sticking out. She pulled the cigarette from her lips.

"Honey, don't no Antoine live here. I just moved in here about a month ago."

"Oh, okay. I'm sorry to bother you."

The woman looked at Summer from head to toe. Then she looked down the street at the guy who was still waving his hands. The lady let out a little giggle.

"You don't look like you from around here." She looked back down the street and said, "Little girl, you wayyyyy outta yo league, baby. I don't know who Antoine is, and why he's so important that you came over here lookin' for him, but you better get outta here and go back where you came from."

"Uhhh, okay. Thanks anyway." Summer took heed to her warning and without hesitation turned around and jogged down the steps. As she ran to her car, she was still watching the guy down the street with her peripheral vision. He looked like a stick figure jumping up and down and still yelling.

"Hey, Shawty! You lookin' good, girl. Why don't you come on down here? I just wanna talk to you for a minute. Come on, girrrlll! I know you hear me."

The guys with him laughed and were falling all over one another.

Whew! I made it. Summer was relieved she'd made it to her car, but continued to look at the crazed guy from the corner of her eye. She was very careful not to give him direct eye contact but was still looking in his direction while she pointed her key toward the car so she could unlock it. Her hand hit someone.

Summer jumped and let out a loud gasp as someone jumped in front of her and leaned up against her car.

"I didn't mean to scare you, girl." Dre was standing in front of her.

Summer was not happy at all to see him, but she was relieved to at least see a face she recognized. She let out a deep breath and held her hand on her chest. "You scared me."

"I didn't mean to scare you, Mama."

Mama? I am not your Mama, she wanted to say but making an enemy with the only person she sort of knew in this neighborhood might not have been such a good idea.

"I've never seen you around here. What are you doing here?"

"I'm looking for a friend." She tried to keep her response brief hoping to avoid a long conversation.

"A friend? Up there?" Dre asked. He was pointing toward where Antoine used to live.

"Yes."

Dre now had a curious look on his face. "Who's your friend?"

"His name is Antoine."

"Antoine! That scrub that used to live up there?"

"I've gotta go. Would you please move so I can get in my car?" She hoped Dre would get the message that she wasn't interested in talking to him and move out of her way.

Ignoring her, he went on, "So that weak punk Antoine is your boy?" He laughed. "What? You mean he cut out without telling you he was leaving? That's messed up. He did leave all fast in the middle of the night, but he could have at least told his girl he was leaving. See, I would never do you like that if you were my girl."

"I'm not his girl. I'm his friend. Now will you please move?" Summer was very agitated by the way Dre was talking about Antoine, but at the same time she was curious what he might know about where Antoine was. She decided to play it cool to see what information she could get from him.

"So you said he left. Do you know where he went?"

"Naw. I just know things got heavy and next thing everybody knew, he was gone. Why are we wasting time talking about that scrub? Let's talk about me and you hooking up. I mean, can I take you to a movie or something?" He reached toward her hair.

Summer pushed his hand away and took a step back.

"Why you being hard, girl?"

"I'm not being hard. I'm just not interested. And aren't you going out with Monique anyway?"

"Who?"

Summer turned up her lips. "Monique." She raised her voice slightly with a bit of sarcasm. "The one who has been acting crazy with me all week. Because of *you*."

He laughed. "Awww, Monique. I'm not going out with her. She's not my type. She's too," he paused, "average. I mean she's alright, but I like girls with class, that are cool and laid back. Someone who will cheer for me and will have my back at the games. Someone who will look good on my arm when we're hangin' out after the game. Kinda like you."

"Well, that's not me. And I can't tell you're not dating her by how she's been acting. Will you please let me get in my car?" Summer stepped to the side of him, gesturing that she wanted him to move. He didn't budge.

"Man, it looks like the lady wants to get in her car," a tall, well-built guy said as he walked up the sidewalk toward them. "Why don't you get out of her way?"

"Why you in my business?" Dre responded, walking over to the guy.

The guy didn't back down. He was much taller and heavier than Dre and didn't seem like he'd have a problem challenging him if that's where he wanted to take the matter.

He stepped toward Dre and raised his voice. "I'm not in ya business bruh, but what kinda dude keeps sweatin' a lady that don't want to be bothered? That game is weak."

While they were arguing Summer unlocked her car door and hurried inside. She locked the doors immediately and took off in a hurry.

"Whew!" She was relieved to be in her car. Her hands were shaking on the steering wheel. Although she was finally in her car, she still wouldn't feel safe until she was out of the apartment complex. She was still watching the people on each side of the street as she left.

"Aww Shawty! Why you leave?" The skinny guy was still yelling and was now jumping up and down waving his arms as she drove past. The guys with him were now laughing uncontrollably. She looked forward as if she didn't see him.

As she left, the same groups of people were assembled. She heard loud talking, laughter, and profanity through her closed window. She glanced at them and had to do a double take. *"No way!"* Stunned, she gripped the steering wheel with her wet, clammy hands. She couldn't believe her eyes.

CHAPTER 17

Big Momma

BIG MOMMA WAS sitting in her favorite chair doing her daily ritual—talking on the phone to her friend Erma about Oprah's newest show on the OWN Network they'd watched earlier that morning.

"I couldn't believe it when that girl was talking about going off the air after twenty-five years. I didn't know what we were going to watch when she went off TV." She paused. "I told you then, can't nobody top what she's done. Noooobody," she said, shaking her head. "Ummm hmm, chile. I know what you mean."

Big Momma sat up in her chair at the sound of the door opening and turned to see who was coming in the house. Summer walked in the door. Big Momma looked at the clock. "Well Erma, I gotta go. My grandbaby's home from school." She paused. "All right. I'll talk to you tomorrow. Bye." She hung up the phone. "Hi, baby."

Summer dropped her keys on the floor. "Hi, Big Momma." She nervously picked them up. Instead of stopping to sit down at the table with Big Momma to talk like usual, she walked toward her bedroom.

"Baby, it's a little late. Where have you been? I was worried about you."

"I'm sorry. I had to stay after school to work on a special project, and then I had to drop off Jazz at home." Summer turned her head and looked away from Big Momma. She hated lying to her.

This chile won't even look me in my eye. "Aren't you going to sit down and talk to Big Momma?"

Without turning around, Summer responded, "I've got a lot of homework and my head is hurting. I'm sorry, Big Momma. Maybe later."

"Okay." Big Momma decided to let it go but she wasn't buying Summer's story for a minute. She watched Summer disappear down the hallway into her bedroom.

Big Momma shook her head and said out loud to no one in particular, "Let me cook this chile some dinner." She headed toward the kitchen and started pulling out cast iron skillets and heavy pots.

An hour and a half later, Big Momma was humming to the tune of *Jesus is on the Main Line* as she stirred fried apples smothered with sugar popping from a large black cast iron skillet. The sweet aroma filled the room. Once Big Momma knew the apples were just right, she turned off the fire under the skillet. She then turned her attention to another skillet that contained crispy fried chicken. She removed the top still covered with condensation dripping into the skillet and she turned over each piece one by one.

"Ahhh!" She was satisfied that the chicken had the golden brown look she wanted. Her dinner was coming along perfectly. The collard greens were already done and the cornbread was ready to come out of the oven. The only thing left was the bread pudding that was ready to go in the oven and the lemon sauce to top it off was simmering on the stove. Big Momma could taste it already. "Mmm," she said aloud as she continued to prepare her meal. *This dinner will bring Summer around and get her talking about whatever it is that's bothering her.* Big Momma's dinners always had a way of healing the family. As she moved along the kitchen wearing her loose fitting, button down the front, flower print dress, she thought, *Hmmph, I'm still healing myself. I miss David so much.* She opened the oven to check her cornbread.

Big Momma realized that ever since David was murdered, the pain she thought had gone away many, many years ago had come back with a vengeance. Her mind took her back to a cold winter night in 1936 in Alabama. She was only 8-years-old when her own father was brutally thrown on a railroad track and murdered for hitting a white man at work that spit in his face.

Big Momma wiped her tears. The pain was as fresh and agonizing as she remembered it almost seventy years ago. That dark dreary night was clear in her mind as if it happened yesterday. Her own pain from the loss of her father was why she understood so well what Summer was feeling. She had to push past her own pain of losing her sweet David and her daddy for Summer and Simone's sake.

Cooking always brought Big Momma comfort. It's what she needed at that time. The kitchen had been her mother's safe haven and was hers as well. It was where for so many years she was able to stir up many happy memories for her family. For now, it served as her therapy.

"Summer sweetie. Dinner is ready." She waited. No sound from Summer.

"Summer?"

"Coming, Big Momma," Summer said groggily.

Five minutes later, Summer dragged herself into the kitchen yawning into her hand with lines imprinted on her face from her pillow.

"Baby, you must have been tired?"

"Yes, Big Momma."

Big Momma pulled out the chair next to her at the table. "Come on and sit down. It looks like you had a long day. Tell me how school was today." She stuck a fork in a chicken breast and placed it on Summer's plate.

Summer picked up the spoon and scooped some greens on her plate. "Hmmm? It was okay."

"Just *okay*? Since when did school become just okay?"

The phone rang. Summer jumped out of her chair and snatched the telephone. "Hello."

She paused for a moment. Then with a puzzled look on her face she pulled the phone from her ear and looked at the receiver before hanging it up.

"Who was it, baby?"

"It was the wrong number."

Just as Summer was almost back to her seat, the phone rang again. She turned back to answer it once again.

"Uh uh." Big Momma shook her head. "You eat your dinner. I'll get the phone." Big Momma got out of her seat and went to the phone.

"Hello." Big Momma held the receiver to her ear. She paused. "Hello?"

"Who was that, Big Momma?" Simone said, walking through the door weighed down with a large black and tan bag on one shoulder, her purse on the other one, and two paper bags full of groceries in her arms.

"Hmmm. I don't know. They hung up," Big Momma said while hanging up the phone.

"That's strange. Someone called a few times last night and held the phone then hung up," Simone said. A few apples fell from the grocery bags she was balancing.

"Let me take one of those bags for you." Big Momma reached to help her.

"I've got it," Simone responded as she made her way to the kitchen counter and dropped the bags down. She let out a sigh of relief.

"Girl, stop treating me like I'm fragile and let me help you some time. Just 'cause I'm old don't mean I can't handle a bag of groceries."

Frustrated, Big Momma threw her hand in the air at Simone then turned to sit back down next to Summer to finish dinner. Before she could sit down, she noticed that Summer was wrapping aluminum foil over her plate.

"Summer, what are you doing? You didn't eat anything."

"I ate a little bit. I'm just not that hungry. I'm sorry." She stuck the plate in the refrigerator. "It was really good though. I'm going to eat the rest later."

"Okay," Big Momma said. She was disappointed that Summer hadn't eaten but she was also concerned that she didn't have enough time to talk to Summer about why she'd been down even more since school started. *She was so excited to go back. We were sure that's what it would take to help lift her spirits after David's death but she's even more in the dumps.*

Picking up a piece of chicken and taking a bite, Simone said with a mouthful, "Summer, Big Momma cooked all of your favorite things. Are you feeling okay? You never turn down this meal."

"I'm okay. I'm just not hungry right now."

Summer kissed Big Momma on her cheek. "I love you, Big Momma."

"I love you too, baby."

Summer headed toward her room.

"When is that concert you and Jasmine are going to?" Simone yelled.

She kept walking. "It's tomorrow night," she responded, loud enough for her mom to hear her.

Once Summer was out of sight Big Momma said, "Something's going on with that chile besides her grieving David's death."

"I think you're right. She seems to be slipping further and further away and she won't talk at all. That's not like her. I'm beginning to really worry about her."

"Let's just keep an eye on her, baby, and keep praying. God is faithful."

CHAPTER 18

Summer

"O-M-G! That was so fun! And Trey Songz was so cute," Jasmine was saying for the tenth time in the past fifteen minutes since the concert had ended. "That's it. It's settled. I'm officially in love. He's *going* to be my husband."

"Jazz, stop dreamin'."

"I'm serious. I will be the wife at every concert behind the scene running all the groupies away."

"You mean the ones like you?" Summer laughed. "Girl, you are crazy. Can you stop walking so slow and come on so we can get to the car and get home before my mom starts calling."

"Well, at least I made you laugh. You act like you didn't have a good time."

"I did. I had a good time. Now come on. We gotta go." Summer turned to walk away but not before she pulled Jasmine by the arm, hoping she'd stop talking and get to the car. She knew this was going to be a long night. Jasmine was staying all night at her house and she was hyped up.

Jasmine jumped in front of her and stood with her feet planted on the sidewalk and her hand on her hip.

"You sure didn't act like you had a good time." She rolled her neck and continued, "Sitting there the whole time like you were somewhere besides a loud concert with that fine Trey Songz. The concert we've been dying to go to since we knew he was coming to town. Some way to show appreciation after all that hard work I put in to win those tickets for us on the radio with my mad music skills."

Summer couldn't help but smile because she knew Jasmine would go on and on. "Okay. You stand there fussing at me if you want to. I'm getting in my car and I'm going home." Summer turned and headed down the street.

"You better not leave me. Let's stop by McDonald's before we go home." She was still dragging along. Summer stopped and looked at Jasmine. She wondered how she could eat another bite. At the concert she'd stuffed herself with chili and jalapeno covered nachos, popcorn and a thirty-two ounce Coke.

"Then you really better come on and walk a little faster because I'm tired," she responded flatly. She was relieved they were almost to her car, but frustrated that Jasmine kept lollygagging around.

"Ughh today, Jazz, today." Summer was beginning to wonder if Jasmine could even walk at another speed. She reached out and pulled her arm again. This time Jasmine's purse fell to the ground and all of her personal belongings scattered all over the sidewalk. Summer watched as Jasmine dropped to her knees picking up her array of belongings that included lipstick, mascara, gum, and an opened pack of peanut M&M's. Summer stooped down to help her. She picked up a bottle of lotion,

Jasmine's student ID, and a box of laxatives. *Laxatives?* Summer held the box up with a frown on her face.

"Jazz, why do you have this?"

"Uh, I've just been constipated lately." She grabbed the box from Summer's hand and stuffed it into her purse.

"Can't you just eat some greens, apples, or something like that?" Summer said as she dropped the other items into Jasmine's purse.

Jasmine gave her a cross look and laughed.

Summer giggled and stood up. "Can we go now?" She turned and walked away.

"Wait up," Jasmine yelled, trying to keep up with Summer's fast pace.

An hour later they'd finally made it home. Summer fell backwards on her bed. *I am glad to be home.* She lay down, sunk her head into her pillow, and closed her eyes.

Jasmine sat down at Summer's desk. She turned on Summer's iPad and logged onto Facebook. "I'm gonna change my post. That concert was wussup!"

Summer opened her eyes. *Here we go again.* She closed her eyes again and tried to ignore Jasmine. Jasmine was obviously ignoring her as well, because she went on humming to her favorite song.

Hoping to block out Jasmine's off tune humming, she snatched the pillow from under her head and shoved it on top of her face.

"What? That…Ugh!" Jasmine yelled at the iPad screen.

Summer opened her eyes and sprang straight up on the bed throwing the pillow to the floor. "What now? What are you yelling about?"

"Look at what that heifer Monique posted on your wall."

"What?" Summer said. Her frustration turned to curiosity and a bit of nervousness. She jumped off the bed and walked over to the desk and looked over Jasmine's shoulder.

"Look." Jasmine pointed to the computer screen.

U must think I'm playin' wit u rich girl! I thought I made myself clear n da hood. Don't think your friend Jazz can save u. I hope you like lotsa different colors. ROFL!!!

"Aww! Is that supposed to be a threat? I'll show that skank who I can save. I can't stand her! I don't know why you didn't let me bash her in the face the other day when she was talkin' crazy."

"I can't stand her either, but there's no use in you getting in trouble because she doesn't like me."

"Forget that. She's just messing with you because she thinks you're a punk. But what she don't know is I got your back and you don't have to worry about her because I got you."

Summer knew Jasmine meant every word that she said. Although Jasmine and her mom moved as things got better for them, she used to live in the projects, just like Monique and Antoine. Jasmine had a small, petite frame that was even thinner than usual, but had no problem fighting anybody that got in her way or in the way of the people she cared about. Everyone knew it. Especially Monique.

"Jazz, it's okay."

"Summer, it's *not* okay. Why do you keep letting her push you around like that?"

Summer could tell Jasmine was very frustrated. "I don't know. It's just too much going on with losing my dad. Then Antoine is nowhere to be found. I just don't feel like dealing with Monique and all her mess. I'm just tired, Jazz. I thought going back to school would help me get my mind off things with my dad, but things have only gotten worse." She went back and sat on the edge of her bed. Her eyes were watering. Jasmine sat down next to her and put her arm around her shoulder.

"I'm sorry. I didn't mean to make you feel bad. I shouldn't have asked you that. I just hate seeing her push you around. Well, like I said, don't worry about her anyway. I'll take care of Monique."

"Jazz." Summer looked at Jasmine with a pleading expression.

"Anyway." Jasmine rolled her eyes and walked back to the desk, sat down, and picked the iPad back up. "What did she mean about making herself clear in the hood?"

"Shhh!" Summer put her finger up to her mouth. "I don't want my mom to hear you," she said in a lower voice. "I'll tell you but you can't say anything to *anybody* and definitely don't mention it around my mom or Big Momma. Okay?"

"Okay, okay. What is it?" Jasmine got back up and went over to the bed again and sat with her legs crossed Indian style facing Summer. She watched her intently, anticipating what she'd hear next.

"I went over to Antoine's apartment looking for him the other day."

"You what?" Jasmine yelled.

"Shhh! I told you to not to talk so loud." Summer put her finger to her lips.

"You know you're not supposed to go over there," Jasmine whispered. "Anyway. Did you see him?"

"No. When I went to his apartment some lady answered the door. He moved away."

"What? Dang!" Jasmine looked confused. "He just moved and didn't say anything to us? That is crazy."

"I know."

"But what does that have to do with Monique?" She looked puzzled.

"As I was leaving, I saw Monique. She was standing on the street with a bunch of people. She looked at me real crazy and was hitting her fist in the palm of her hand. I guess that was her way of saying she was going to fight me."

Jasmine's face grimaced. "I can't stand her. Well, she was right about one thing."

"What's that?"

"That it's not over. I'm going to get her."

"Jazz." Summer scolded.

"And what did she mean about she hopes you like a lot of different colors?" Jasmine continued, ignoring her plea.

"I don't know what that crazy girl is talking about. I don't even want to talk about her anymore." She put her pillow back on her face and lay down.

"Ummm hmmm," Jasmine said.

The room fell silent.

Maybe Jazz finally calmed down. Now maybe I can rest and hopefully forget about crazy Monique.

The longer Summer laid there, the harder she tried, but couldn't get Monique off her mind. She began to pray silently. *God, why am I going through this? What did I do to deserve this? I know I'm not perfect but I'm not all that bad either. I know people that don't even know you, God, that don't go through all I've gone through. I lost my daddy. That's the worst thing that's ever happened to me. Now it seems that I've lost one of my best friends. I don't know if Antoine is okay or not. But if all of that wasn't enough God, you send Monique to torment me. Why? Why can't she see that I have no interest in that boy, Dre? And then I'm worried that Jasmine will get herself in trouble at school for fighting by trying to defend me. I don't want her to get put out of school. God, when will this all end? I've never doubted that you were there for me, but things are really crazy. Crazier than they've ever been. If you are still there will you please let me know? Amen.*

The room was still silent. Wondering why Jasmine had gotten so quiet, Summer opened her eyes and looked over at her. Jasmine was turned away from the desk hunched over holding her stomach.

"Jazz! What's wrong with you?"

"Nothing." She sat up with a frown on her face. "I'm just having cramps in my stomach. I'll be right back." She jumped out of the chair and rushed down the hallway to the bathroom. Summer heard her abruptly turning the doorknob back and forth and then she heard knocking.

"Is somebody in there?" Jasmine pleaded.

Summer stared up at her ceiling. *She sure is using the bathroom a lot lately. I guess it's from all that food she's been eating or maybe she took one of those laxatives she had in her purse and it's starting to work.*

"I'm in here. Give me a minute," Summer heard her mom yell back at Jasmine. She didn't think Jasmine would be able to hold it if she didn't get in there pretty soon.

Nearly ten minutes later Summer realized Jasmine still hadn't come back from the bathroom. She stood up.

"Jazz, how long does it take to use the bathroom?" Summer yelled. She walked into the hallway toward the bathroom.

"I'll be there in a minute. My stomach is still hurting," Jasmine yelled back.

As Summer walked toward the bathroom she saw her mother standing with her ear to the bathroom door.

"Shhh," Simone said to Summer with her finger on her lips.

"What are you doing?" Summer said in a whisper.

"*Shhh,*" her mother commanded.

"Why are we whispering?" Summer asked as she walked down the hallway and stood in front of her mother. She could hear Jasmine gagging in the bathroom.

Confused as to why her mother was just standing there listening while Jasmine was clearly not feeling well, Summer whispered, "Is she okay?" She stepped toward the door with her hand extended to reach for the doorknob.

Simone blocked her hand. Summer stopped but was still very confused with her mother's unusual behavior.

The sound of Jasmine gagging on the other side of the door made Summer feel sick to her stomach. She watched her mom with her ear still to the door. She didn't seem grossed out in the least by the obnoxious vomiting sound. Suddenly the gagging stopped. The next sound they heard was that of the toilet flushing followed by running water. Jasmine's footsteps could be heard walking toward the door. Simone removed her ear from the door but still stood in front of it.

What is she doing? Summer thought.

The bathroom door swung open. Jasmine was clearly startled. She jumped backward after seeing Simone standing in front of her. Summer caught Jasmine's eye as she looked nervously past Simone. Summer shrugged her shoulders. "Uhhh, excuse me," she said politely as she stepped to the left of Simone attempting to walk around her. Simone stepped to the side still in front of Jasmine blocking her from walking past.

"Jasmine, are you okay, honey?"

"Yes, ma'am. I..." She looked at Summer. "I feel a lot better now. I've been constipated and I was finally able to use the bathroom."

Simone frowned. "But Jasmine, you were vomiting." Without giving Jasmine a chance to keep making excuses she continued, "When I left the bathroom I heard you stop at the door. You were obviously listening to see if I was away from the door. Of course that made me curious so I stood there for a few minutes. That's when I heard you gagging. I need you to tell me what's going on." Simone put her arm on Jasmine's shoulder.

"Oh, that." She laughed, throwing her hand in the air like it was no big deal. "My stomach was just a little upset. Like I said, I haven't been able to use the bathroom and I finally could. For some reason my stomach was upset and I had to throw up. That's it." She threw both hands up and shrugged. "That's all. It's really no big deal. I'm okay, Mrs. M."

Simone wasn't buying it. "Jasmine. This is very serious. I've been watching you for the past several months."

"I don't understand what you mean, Mrs. M."

"I've watched you eat until you were stuffed to no end. Then you usually head to the bathroom like clockwork every time you're done eating. You have spent more time in the bathroom in the past months than the entire time I've known you. Honey, you have very clear signs of bulimia."

Jasmine looked scared and confused.

"I've seen children at school time and time again with the same eating disorder."

"Oh, no! It's nothing like that. I just—"

"Jasmine. I care enough about you to help you get this thing under control before it's too late."

Too late! What's going on now with Jasmine? Summer thought.

"If you don't stop this now, this could lead to your teeth rotting and damage to your throat from sticking your finger in it to make yourself vomit."

Summer's mouth fell open from shock. She couldn't believe what she was hearing.

Simone continued, "Jasmine, so much can happen to you by doing this. You can even die, sweetheart. Do you realize that?"

Jasmine looked down and her shoulders dropped in defeat. "No, ma'am."

"We need to first call your mother. I'll help you all get help for this. You really need to speak with someone about this. It's a serious problem."

"Can you just not tell my mom about this? I promise I'll stop. I can do it on my own. I don't need help."

"Jasmine, honey, first of all, I'd be less of a parent myself to know something like this was going on with you and not tell your mother. She deserves to know that you're having this problem. She'd be heartbroken if she realized you were hurting and she didn't know about it. Secondly, this is not the type of thing you should even attempt to resolve on your own. There are professional people that will help you through this. I promise you. Everything will be fine."

Summer stared at her best friend looking defeated and afraid. *Now this. God, I really do hope things will get better. I'm still waiting for you to show me you're there.*

CHAPTER 19

Simone

"I can't thank you enough for finding someone who could help Jasmine. You know I love her like she's my own daughter," Simone said, facing Vivian who was driving out of the parking lot of their favorite Italian restaurant.

"Simone, if you thank me one more time…" Vivian said with a chuckle.

"I know, I know. I've thanked you probably a thousand times, but it just meant so much to me that you were able to find someone who could help so fast. It meant even more to her mother. She was shocked beyond belief. She had no idea what was going on with Jasmine."

"That's what friends are for. It's unbelievable the stress these kids must have on them today."

"Tell me about it. I wouldn't want to grow up in today's world," Simone said, sighing deeply. "Now I've got Jasmine taken care of. If I could figure out what's going on with my own daughter, then maybe I'd be okay." Her voice sank.

"What's wrong with Summer? I mean, besides losing David, of course."

"I don't know. She comes home and goes straight to her bedroom. When she is around us she's really quiet. She only speaks if we drum up the conversations. She almost seems depressed, V."

"Hmmm."

"Something's going on and I just can't put my finger on it. She was even more down after all of that happened to Jasmine. Then Monday rolled around and she said she was too sick to go to school. She didn't have a fever but I didn't want to push her so she's been out all this week." Simone's heart sank. "You would think after working with other people's children for close to twenty years and solving everyone else's problems, I might be able to help my own kid."

"Come on now. Don't be so hard on yourself, Simone. Sometimes it is easier to see problems when it is other people's children. The closer you are to the situation the harder it is sometimes to see what's going on. Stop beating yourself up. You're a great mother. I know lots of kids who would do anything for a mother who's remotely close to the way you are. Give yourself a break." Vivian turned onto Simone's street.

"I know. Maybe I am beating myself up a little too much but—"

"But nothing." Vivian reached over and grabbed Simone's hand. "You're an awesome mother and don't forget it."

Simone looked at Vivian and smiled. "Okay. I receive that. Thanks."

"No thanks needed. You keep your head up. This too shall pass," Vivian said as she turned into Simone's driveway. "You let me know if there is anything I can do to help you with Summer. I know it's—"

"Uhhh!" Simone gasped.

"What's wrong?"

"Look!" Simone managed to get out as she pointed toward Summer's car sitting in the driveway where it always sat. Their two car garage was reserved for Simone's car and David's that was parked in the same place since his death.

"Oh my gosh! What in the world?" Vivian replied.

"Who could have done this?" Simone yelled as she jumped out of the car and ran up to Summer's car that used to be black, but had been spray painted with blue, red, orange, green, and turquoise spray paint.

"Simone, someone she knows had to do this. Look at the message on the windshield," Vivian said.

The message on the windshield written in red spray paint read, *It ain't over, Rich Girl.*

Simone gasped with her hand to her mouth. "That's a threat. I need to ask Summer what's going on." She headed toward the front door.

Vivian stood in the driveway. "I'll call the police. You need to file a report," she said.

Simone couldn't unlock the door and get into the house fast enough. As soon as the door flew open she yelled, "Summer!" In the back of her mind she was worried that someone may have come in the house and hurt her.

"What's going on out here?" Big Momma inquired, coming from the kitchen carrying a spatula.

"Yes, Mom. What's wrong?" Summer came out of her room with a puzzled look on her face.

"Summer, someone spray painted all over your car. Did you know there was someone here? Did either of you hear them outside?"

"Lawd have mercy. I didn't hear anyone. What else can happen to this family?" Big Momma shook her head and went back in the kitchen.

"What? No, I didn't hear anyone either." She ran outside to her car. When she came back inside, Simone could see by her face that she was clearly upset, but didn't seem as shocked as she and Vivian were. Simone's wheels began to turn. *Summer knows who did this.*

Simone looked her directly in her eyes. "Summer, do you know who did this?"

Summer hesitated, but responded, "I think I do."

"You think? Who do you *think* did this?"

"There's a girl at school who's been talking crazy to me and trying to start stuff with me."

"Summer, how could you let something like this go on and not tell me? How long has this been going on?"

"Since school started."

"Since school started? Summer!"

Summer looked at the floor then went over and sat on the couch.

"Who is this girl or should I say *thug*? What's her name?"

"Her name is Monique."

"I've never heard of her. This doesn't make sense. You don't usually have problems with people. Why would she do something like this?"

"Do you remember that day me and Jazz went to Di Maio's?"

"Yes, I remember. Before school started?"

"Yes. Well there was this guy there named Dre who was with Monique. I guess he was with her but he was all up in my face. I wasn't thinking about him but I guess she really likes him and instead of getting mad at him she got mad at me. She knocked my drink over on me. I thought it may have been an accident but ever since we got back to school, she's been talking crazy to me. She left a message on my Facebook page that she hoped I liked a lot of different colors. I guess that's what she meant. She was planning to spray paint my car."

"She threatened you on Facebook?"

"Yes, ma'am."

"How stupid. That girl seems like real trash. What kind of parents does she have doing this kind of stuff to people and their personal property? How old is this little…girl?"

"She's a year older than me and Jazz. She's 17-years-old."

"I'd bet picking on kids younger than her is something she does often." As Simone ranted, her mind began to race. "Has she hit you or hurt you physically in any way?"

"Well, she started out by bumping into me and she did end up hitting me one day. Jazz jumped in and pushed her. That's when she told me it's not over."

Simone understood now what was going on. Summer had been bullied and Jasmine had been defending her. Now with Jasmine out of school, away at the in-patient treatment center for her bulimia, Summer, was afraid to go back to school, so this thuggish girl came to her. To *their* home. Simone wasn't about to take this. Her head was pounding.

"Don't you worry. She won't be bothering you anymore. I promise you that. But honey, why didn't you tell me about this?"

"I'm sorry, Mom. I know you always tell me that I can talk to you about anything and I know that I can, but I was kind of embarrassed. But mostly, I didn't want to worry you. You've had enough going on with…" she paused, "…with Daddy and all."

"Summer, we all have had a lot going on with your daddy dying. And you were embarrassed? You don't ever have to be embarrassed to tell me anything. That girl is a bully and you shouldn't have had to go through that alone. I'm glad Jazz was there for you, but I'm still your mother. You have to let me help you through these kinds of things. That's what I'm here for. Daddy would have wanted you to let me help you with this. Especially since he's not here."

"I know, Mom, but—"

Vivian walked in the door. "Simone, the policeman is here. He's looking at the car. Can you come out? He wants to talk with you and Summer."

"Sure. Summer, come on." They went outside where the young officer was walking around the car while writing on a notepad.

"Hello, Officer. I'm Simone McClain."

"Yes, ma'am." He reached to shake her hand. "It's a pleasure to meet you. I knew your husband. He was an awesome man."

"Thank you."

"I'm really sorry this happened to your car."

"Yes. I am too. I'm even more concerned because this is my daughter's car. What's even more troubling is that she and my mother-in-law were at home when this happened."

"Did either of them see who did this?"

"No. They had no idea it even happened. I saw it a little bit ago when I drove up with my friend. But my daughter was just telling me that she thinks she knows who did it though."

Vivian looked at Summer oddly. "You think you know who did this?"

"I'm pretty sure I do." Summer went on to explain everything to the officer that had been going on with Monique.

"We take this very seriously. I've got everything you've said in my report. Again, I'm really sorry about this. If you happen to talk with any of your neighbors and find that someone saw something and can give a description or identify the person, please call us back."

"We certainly will. Thank you, Officer." Simone reached over and pulled Summer into her arms into a tight embrace. She wondered what happened that stopped her from being able to protect her little girl. She continued to hold her as she looked at Vivian over Summer's shoulder.

Vivian raised her eyebrows and looked at Simone who said, "I'll call you later. I have an excruciating headache and I'm going to take a nap."

"Yeah, you go and take a nap. I'm going back to my office to make a few calls to some of my friends. In the meantime, let me know if there's anything else I can do. Bye, Summer."

"Bye, Aunt Vivian."

Simone and Summer went back in the house where Big Momma was sitting in her chair in the family room. Simone turned to Summer. "I hate it's so late. I can't call the school until tomorrow but I will take care of this first thing in the morning." She looked at Summer for what felt like a few minutes. Simone's heart broke, but she couldn't worry about how she felt. She wanted Summer to know that she was safe and that she would take care of this.

"It'll be okay. I promise."

"Okay, Mom." Simone could see Summer's concern. Summer forced a smile and went to her room.

Simone looked at Big Momma and shook her head. "Can you believe this?"

"No, baby, I can't."

"I feel awful that this has been going on and I had no idea. A parent is supposed to protect their child. I need to protect Summer from this wild girl that obviously has no home training. I have no time to waste. I've seen these bully situations far too many times. There's no way I'm going to let my daughter become a teen statistic that will be scarred for the rest of her life by a bully or even worst, get killed by the bully. Or be like that girl, Megan, at Summer's school who took her own life because of feeling she had nowhere to turn. I have to handle this quickly and in a way that Summer won't feel bad about going back to school." Simone had an excruciating headache. She sat on the couch hoping to take a short nap but she couldn't stop worrying. Eventually, she drifted off to sleep.

Simone's head was relaxed on the back cushion of the tan leather couch in her family room. She realized she had fallen asleep. She sat up and looked at the clock. *Had an hour gone past that quick?* She looked across the room into her dining room at the pile of bills sitting on the table that needed her attention. She let her head drop back on the couch. The bills could wait five more minutes. For the past hour she was actually comfortable and was able to forget about all of the craziness that had been going on in her life lately.

After a few minutes, she dragged herself up and walked over to the table in the dining room where her laptop sat open. She sat in the chair in front of her laptop and watched her screensaver, a picture of her family on vacation on the beach of Miami. *Wow, things were so normal then. That was before our lives were turned upside down.* For a brief moment while looking at the picture, she could feel the tension leave her body and she relaxed. An easy smile came across her face. She looked at Summer standing in between her and David in the photo. *Summer was so happy then. So was I. I miss David so much.* Simone closed her eyes. *God I know you will not put more on us than we can bear. I know I've asked you over and over again but I'm coming to you again. Please get us through all that's going on, Lord.*

She opened her eyes and looked at David in the picture with his usual, beautiful smile. It always made her feel warm inside. She remembered how he made her feel loved and protected. She knew all the drama with this bully wouldn't be going on if he was there. Simone looked away from their images on the laptop and turned her attention to all of the papers spread across the table, piled into several different stacks according to when they were due. The stress eased back in causing her shoulders to feel tight.

How did David do this? How did he keep all of this straight without ever missing a due date? He was a stickler for paying bills and he had a routine. Simone never bothered to learn it because he always insisted that caring for the bills and the family was his responsibility and he never complained. He made it seem so easy. Well, nothing seemed routine or easy anymore. This was her new normal. On top of working every day and now taking care of all the bills alone, she was also feeling the pinch of less money coming into their home. Overall, she felt blessed that she was able to still maintain all of their expenses on just her teaching salary. Without a doubt things were definitely tighter than they used to be and she had to now budget differently than before. She knew it would get better when she got the sizeable lump sum of money from David's death insurance and his pension from the police department but it took a very long time for all of that to be processed. But for now she thanked God for keeping them on what they had.

David always was an awesome provider from day one. Simone remembered back to when they were first married and how she had insisted that she was going to remain a working woman. She insisted that she was as much a part of the family they were planning to begin as David and she too wanted to contribute. He was adamant that he was the man of the house and it was his job to take care of the family and their expenses. Simone was head strong and would not give in. After they went around and around they finally agreed that Simone would take care of the expense of groceries and basic household items. When Summer came, she bought things Summer needed and those cute little things a mom enjoyed buying for her little girl. David made it clear that he really wanted Simone to keep her money for herself but this was the compromise he agreed to in order to keep the peace.

Thinking about David and their early years of marriage made her very sad. She'd heard that time heals the pain but her heart still ached. David was the only man she'd ever loved and it still didn't seem right that he was gone.

She was distracted by Joy London from Channel 7 News whose voice came through the speakers of her flat screen television with a special report. *Breaking News. Another teenager was found dead today on the south side on Normal Street. Police say that the victim was shot several times but they believe the single* gunshot wound to the head was more than likely the one that killed him. The victim's name has not yet been released and his family has not yet been reached. Stay tuned as we continue to keep you updated as the details of this case continues to unfold. This is Joy London reporting on the scene. Channel 7ABC news.

"Hmmm, that's a shame," Simone said out loud to no one in particular. Her eyes welled up with tears. It baffled her how the crime rate continued to rise. It was normal in Chicago to hear of people being murdered every day, but when David was killed it became personal. She thought about the mother of that young boy and the heartache she must be feeling when she hears her child was killed in cold blood, at the hands of someone who had no value for human life. Had the mother expected the news? Had she sat nervously by the phone for years the way she'd waited to hear that David had been killed? No matter how many days she waited by the phone for that dreaded call, nothing could have prepared her for losing David.

The phone rang. It startled Simone and shook her out of her thoughts. She jumped up from the dining room table and walked over to the coffee table in the living room. Trying to compose herself, she lifted the handset and placed it on her ear.

"Hello."

"May I speak with Mrs. Simone McClain?"

"This is Mrs. McClain."

"Hello, ma'am. This is Sergeant Tooley at the Chicago Police Department."

"Yes." Simone sat on the couch.

"We have new developments in your husband's case and we'd like for you, your mother-in-law, and daughter to come down to the station today if any way possible."

Simone felt anxiety come over her. It felt like her throat was closing. She took a deep breath.

"What time do you want us to come down?"

"As soon as possible. We're questioning a couple of people. They're not considered suspects at this time but we feel that they may have information that might be critical to the case. We want you to be here because we'd like to know if you recognize either of them as someone your husband may have known. We believe what they have to say, along with another piece of evidence we've been looking into for months, might be what we need to crack the case."

Simone stood up from the couch and grabbed her purse. "I'll be right there. Thanks." Without saying goodbye she hung up the phone. *Oh my gosh! They might be close to solving the case. Who could these possible suspects be?* The case had been stagnant for so long that deep down inside she had begun to lose hope that they would even find the person who killed David. Her curiosity ran wild.

"Summer?" She paused. "Big Momma?"

Summer ran out of her room and almost collided with Big Momma who came out of the kitchen at the same time.

"Baby, what's wrong?" Big Momma said, wiping her hands on a dish towel.

"Sergeant Tooley just called. He wants us to come down. They're questioning some people and want to know if we might recognize them. They also think they may have important information about David's case. I'm not sure if I can do this." She didn't have the strength to do it alone.

"Baby, don't worry. Big Momma is right by your side all the way."

"Summer. Do you think you can handle it?"

"Mom, I want to go with you."

Simone showed a nervous smile.

"Thanks. I love you both so much. Okay, let's go. He said he wanted us to come right away."

Summer walked quickly back to her room and Big Momma went to her room where they both snatched their purses and returned to the family room. Without looking back, they all headed out the door.

CHAPTER 20

Summer

THE RIDE TO the police station was long and agonizing. It seemed to take much longer than it ever had before. Simone drove nervously while Big Momma sat on the passenger side and Summer sat in the back seat gazing out the window. They were all completely quiet and absorbed in their own thoughts about what this new evidence might be and who could be at the police station that might have information. Up to this point there had never been any witnesses to step forward. Although the community's silence frustrated them, it didn't surprise them. They knew all too well, being the family of a police officer for years, that people in the streets had a code of silence. They did not snitch on one another. They also knew that the average law abiding citizen would be too afraid to speak up.

Summer sat with one arm crossed over the other while she rubbed them to warm herself from the chill she felt. She shifted continuously from side to side in her seat. She was so nervous she didn't know what to do with herself. The coolness she felt caused her to continue fidgeting in her seat. She kept thinking how it would feel to actually have the case solved. She thought about how badly she wanted the horrible animal caught that ended her daddy's life. If anyone deserved to live it was her father. He cared so much for other people. He even cared about losers like the one that killed him. He believed even they had some good in them. Summer always struggled to understand that concept, especially now. With all of these thoughts it just made her even more nervous.

Who could be at the police station? Could this really be the element to crack this case? As nervous as she was about finding out who the police was questioning, and if the information they had would help solve the case, she also wondered how she would feel. Would it make her feel better? Worse? Would she be able to forgive the killer? Could she hate them any more once she was able to put a face with who now was the invisible person she already despised? It was driving her completely insane. She needed to know now. *What is taking us so long to get there?*

Big Momma broke the silence. "Are you babies okay?"

"Yes, ma'am," Summer responded.

"I'm okay, Big Momma. Just feeling a great deal of anxiety about these mystery people the police are questioning that have popped up all of a sudden," Simone admitted.

"I know, baby but you know God is going to get us through this like he has everything else that we've had to deal with."

"You're right. The call was just unexpected. Out of nowhere."

"I know. You just lean on God for strength."

They approached a light at East 111th Street where the police station sat. Although she tried to lean on Big Momma's words—and they did give her a tiny bit of hope—she still found herself trying to suppress the anxiety that was building inside of her.

Simone turned the corner, and right down from the police station, she found a parking spot. She pulled in, put the car in park, and turned off the ignition. Summer heard her take a deep breath as she sat looking through the windshield.

"Are you ready?" Big Momma grabbed Simone's hand and held it.

"I think so." Simone's voice was shaky.

Big Momma turned slightly looking toward the back seat. "Summer, baby, are you ready?"

"Yes, Big Momma." Summer wasn't really sure but figured it was the right thing to say.

"Okay. Well, we know God is with us. So let's go on in and do this."

Without speaking a word, they all opened their doors and got out of the car and began walking toward the large doors of the police station.

Once inside, people were sitting throughout the room. All of them looked as if they'd rather be somewhere else. The officers behind the desk seemed to be all over the place. Some were answering the phones that were ringing constantly. Some were flipping through papers. Other officers were talking to complaining people that were frustrated because they had to wait. Summer even noticed that one officer was talking on the phone, had someone standing at the desk in front of him waiting, and he was drinking what she assumed to be coffee from a mug, all at the same time.

This madness only added to their anxiety. They stood in

front of the door for a few minutes after walking in. Simone tried to figure out who she could talk to without having to wait for the busy officers behind the desk to help her. At that moment she saw a tall, slender officer standing to the left of them getting ready to walk away from a lady who moments ago was yelling about her car being towed. Simone rushed over to him before he had a chance to get busy again. She was close enough that Summer could still hear her.

"Excuse me, sir." The man looked down at her, clearly frustrated. She studied his thin face and looked at his thinning blonde hair. As Summer watched her mom looking up at the man, she imagined by his annoyed expression that he was probably thinking, *Lady, who do you think you are? Wait your turn like everyone else.*

"Yes?" he asked in an aggravated tone.

Simone didn't let his tall, lanky stature and irritated look intimidate her. Before he had a chance to turn her away and direct her to the desk, she spoke quickly and stood tall. "I received a call from Sergeant Tooley who asked me to come here to speak with him. Would you mind letting him know that Mrs. Simone McClain is here to see him?"

Right away his expression turned from frustrated to sympathetic. "Oh, you're Mrs. McClain. Ma'am, I've never had the pleasure of meeting you. I'm Officer Tim Nixon. I worked with your husband for years. I'm so sorry for your loss. He was a wonderful man. There aren't many people like him that I've ever met in my life. We really miss him. I've been keeping your family in my prayers."

Relieved, Simone responded, "Thank you. We really appreciate all the support we've received from the police department."

Officer Nixon said, "I'll get Sergeant Tooley for you. I'll be right back."

"Thank you."

Officer Nixon smiled and quickly turned and walked away. Simone took a deep breath, relieved she had avoided having to wait to be helped. She turned around and walked back over to where Summer and Big Momma was standing.

"He's going to get him. I guess we'll know what's going on shortly." They all looked at one another in expectation.

About five minutes after Officer Nixon left, Summer looked up and saw a man with salt and pepper hair, flawless skin, about six foot one with a medium build and a muscular frame walking toward them. If she hadn't seen him before and recognized him to be Sergeant Tooley she would have had to do a double take because he looked so much like George Clooney. He walked with confidence through the crowd. He approached Simone and gave her a very warm greeting.

"Hello, Mrs. McClain. Thank you for coming down here so quickly."

"No problem," Simone responded.

Sergeant Tooley turned to face Big Momma and Summer. "Hello, ladies."

"Hello," Big Momma and Summer responded.

"If you all would follow me this way we'll get right to it." He pointed toward a door that lead past the crowded work area in front of them, then turned and began walking.

Without saying a word they all followed him. Sergeant Tooley escorted them down a long corridor which led them into a small room. The room felt cold and looked very empty except for the wooden table sitting in the middle of the floor and the six chairs around the table. It reminded Summer of something she'd seen on one of the cop shows on TV. On the table sat two boxes of tissue on each end and a tape recorder. Noticing the tissue, Summer thought, *Tissues on the table. Hmmm? I wonder if he thinks this is going to be emotional to sit through.*

Sergeant Tooley pulled out a chair for Big Momma and then for Simone. They both thanked him and sat down. He went to the other side of the table and pulled out a chair for Summer. She politely thanked him and sat down as well. There was a big glass window that covered one entire wall of the small room. Summer noticed that on the other side of the window was another room. It looked like one of those interrogation rooms she'd seen on *Law and Order*. There was a man sitting in there in plain clothes. He looked so professional in his black dress slacks and a white button down shirt. Summer thought he appeared to be some type of detective. Then she saw that he had a badge on his shirt. That confirmed her thoughts. He was in fact a detective. The man was shuffling through a pile of papers that were in a manila folder and seemed really intent on whatever it was he was looking for in the file.

After they were all sitting down Sergeant Tooley took the seat in front of the tape recorder.

"I want you all to listen to a recording. It's a voicemail Officer McClain left right before he was murdered. Hearing his voice will be difficult, especially considering the circumstances surrounding it." He paused. "I have to warn you, as tough as it will be to hear this, I have to let you listen to it because we consider it to be very critical evidence in the case. There are two other voices on the recording besides his. We believe that one of the people on the recording may have known Officer

McClain. If we can find out who he is, we might have the break we need in solving the case. That's why it's important for each of you to hear it. We need to know if any of you might recognize one or both of the voices. We've kept information about this extremely confidential and have only told a select few people about it before now because of how crucial it is to the case. We didn't want to risk information about it getting leaked out to the media." He paused again and looked around the table at each of the ladies. "Is everyone ready?"

Hesitantly, they all responded, "Yes."

Sergeant Tooley continued, "I want each of you to listen very closely."

They nodded. The room fell silent for a few seconds. Sergeant Tooley reached over to the tape recorder and pushed the button. David's voice rang from the recorder and filled the room.

"*Hey, Jay.*" Summer could tell by Simone's shiver that she felt the same shockwave go through her body that she felt when she heard his voice. The room seemed to have gotten even colder than it was when they walked in earlier.

"*Man, I was hoping you might be out of your appointment by now. I really need to talk to you. You won't believe what just happened at this run I went on. I know I thought it was going to be a simple run but it was anything but that. Now I almost wish you hadn't had that appointment and would have been with me. Man, it was crazy! I actually thought I was going to pass out when I walked in that place. Please call me back as soon as you get this message. I need to talk to you. I know I'm always trying to give you advice but I really need you on this one. I don't say it often enough but you're my best friend and I'm telling you, I can't talk to anyone about this until I talk to you, dude.*" Summer could hear in his voice that whatever had happened clearly bothered him and had him very stressed out.

The distressed look on Big Momma's face showed that her heart was breaking. Big Momma always spoke of how she always wanted to be there to help him through whatever he was going through. David always told her he was a man and he didn't like burdening his mother with his problems. Big Momma didn't care. She always tried to be there anyway.

David's voice spoke again. *"This is crazy! With all the principles I stand for and everything I've ever believed and worked for as a man, I have to wonder how something like this could happen to me. Man, I know I'm rambling on and I probably sound really crazy right now but I just need to talk to you as soon as possible so I can clear this all up in my mind before I go home. I don't know how I'm going to tell Simone this but, what I do know is that I have to talk to her. I have to talk to her, Summer, and Big Momma."*

Summer loved hearing her dad say her name again but it was weird because she knew he was hurting which caused a tugging feeling on her heart. *What in the world happened that had him so torn apart?*

"I feel like I've failed and it's tearing me up." David's voice spoke again through the recorder. Then there was a pause followed by static as if he was moving the phone. *"Man, I have to hang up. I have to handle another situation here and I'll meet you after I grab something to eat, but if you get this message first give me a call. Don't wait man. It's important. Later."* Then his voice faded. It was much more distant, as if he'd moved the phone away from his mouth.

He must have thought he hung up the phone.

"Hey! Hey!" Then there was more static as if he was moving

abruptly. *"Hey, you over there, by the car. I need to speak to you for a minute."*

A male voice spoke. *"What do you need to talk to me about? I'm not bothering anyone."*

David spoke again. *"We've had reports of burglaries in the area. As a matter of fact, I just took a report. Have you heard anything?"*

"Naw, man. You got me messed up. I ain't no snitch. I haven't seen nothin'."

"Hold on. Before you leave, I want to ask you a few more questions," David was heard saying.

"Man, why are you messin' with me? I don't know anything about no burglaries. If I did, I still wouldn't tell you. I already told you I ain't no snitch."

"Actually, I want to ask you about something else. Haven't I seen you before at East High School?"

"What does that have to do with the burglaries around here?"

Summer squinted her eyes frowning and listened closer. *That could be Daddy's killer.* She wanted the person or people that killed him to be found so badly. She wanted to know the voice so they could be caught and pay for killing her father. She'd do anything to see them pay for what they did. She kept listening. *Do I know that voice? It might sound familiar but it's so far away.* Disappointed, she admitted to herself that maybe the voice didn't sound familiar.

David's voice continued to speak. *"I want to ask you about the girl that killed herself at the school."*

"What about that trick?"

"Her name was Megan, and I want to know what you know about the young man that started the lewd picture of her going around the school." David's voice got stern and seemed as if he'd

finally had enough. Summer knew her dad despised it when boys were disrespectful to girls. *"Look, I'm not going to keep playing this game with you. I need you to answer the question."*

The guy spoke again. *"I ain't doin nothin'! Why are you harassing me about that chick? The police already asked me about that anyway, at the school. I already told them I didn't have nothin' to do with that."*

"Well, based on the investigation I've done, I think you do have something to do with it. May I take a look at the cell phone you've got in your hand?"

"Man, I'm not givin' you my phone."

Another more distant voice yelled. *"Man cool out! He's the police but he's all right. He don't give brotha's trouble. Don't do anything stupid."*

The first man's voice yelled back, *"Dude, stay out of this. You a snitch? You work for the police? What! What!"*

"Naw, man. I'm just telling you it's not worth it. Your head is messed up and you're not thinking. You're getting ready to mess up bad. You don't want to get into no mess with a cop over a cell phone."

"Man, you just stay out of this. I got this. I'm sick of these pigs. Especially the snooty one's like him that come down here acting like they better than us, telling people what we don't have to do to make a living and then they go back to their plush homes outside the hood. You don't have to tell me about this cat. I done seen him plenty of times around here actin' like he's a knight in shining armor coming through the hood to save the day. He don't know nothin' about us and why we have to do what we do. Well, I got my pass out the hood and it's not gettin' ready to get messed up over that nasty chick."

David yelled, *"Put your hands up and move away from the car. Take your hands out of your pockets!"*

"Man, why you got your hand on your gun?"

"Dude, do what he say! It's not worth it over a phone. Why don't you just give it to him?" the other guy reasoned.

The first man's said, *"Man, shut up. Mind yo business. This is between me and him."*

David yelled, *"You! Stay over there. I said don't move. Don't move."*

"No," the reasonable man yelled.

Sergeant Tooley reached for the recorder to turn it off but not soon enough. The next sound was that of multiple gun shots. The sound was so loud and piercing. After that there was a loud noise as if the phone hit the ground and then it cut off.

There was a loud scream in the room. It took a few seconds for Summer to realize it was her own voice she heard. She felt as if she was there with her father. She imagined him lying on the ground with blood seeping from his chest while he moaned as the people around him ran away like rats scurrying in the night.

Simone had tears running down her face. She began wiping her tears with the tissue that was sitting on the table.

Big Momma held her chest as if her heart felt like someone was squeezing it. She was holding Simone in a tight embrace. Summer's cries grew louder. She was hyperventilating and she felt like she couldn't breathe. Simone tried to compose herself so that she could comfort Summer. After wiping her tears she walked around the table and sat down next to Summer. She put her arm around her in a tight embrace.

"Are you okay, baby?"

"Yes," Summer muttered through sniffles, attempting to breathe clearly.

"Okay, baby. I'm here with you and so is Big Momma." Big Momma forced a smile attempting to comfort Summer.

"Okay?" Simone pressed.

"Yes," Summer insisted.

"I know this is tough but we have to be strong for Daddy. The police think this is going to help us in getting closer to finding his murderer." *Murderer.* Summer looked at her mother as the word parted her lips. Those words were so hard for Summer to hear. She could see the pain in her mom's face. She knew this was just as hard for her mom to face as it was for her. Summer was beginning to believe that maybe her mom was right. Maybe the police were working really hard and was determined to find his killer. If that was the case she knew her mom was right that they had to be strong and do whatever they could to help even if it meant going through the torture of listening to that terrible tape. She would never rest as long as his killer was walking the streets.

Sergeant Tooley interrupted. "I'm really sorry. I didn't mean for you all to hear the gunshots." He paused. "This is a good time for a break if you need it."

"Do you need a break, sweetie?" Simone asked Summer.

"No, I'm okay." She was beginning to calm down.

"Are you sure?"

Summer nodded.

"It's okay. We'll continue," Simone instructed.

"Okay. Very well. We will continue. Does either of the voices you heard sound familiar at all?" Sergeant Tooley said.

Simone said, "No. They don't."

Big Momma also said they didn't to her.

In Summer's mind she was making herself believe that they might sound familiar but again she thought she was just wanting to know the voices so the killer could be caught. She didn't speak.

Sergeant Tooley asked, "Summer? Do they to you?"

Summer hesitated and then said, "No."

Sergeant Tooley said, "Are you sure?"

Summer responded, "No. I don't recognize any of the voices. I wish I did." She wished the voices weren't so muffled and distant. She would never forget anything she had just heard on that recording for the rest of her life.

"Okay. If any of you think about it later and you think they even sound remotely familiar please call me. Sometimes it comes to people later," Sergeant Tooley explained.

Simone faced him and asked, "Okay. We will definitely call you if anything comes to us. I was wondering though if you have any idea what could have happened on that run that had David so upset before the altercation with the man outside."

"No, ma'am. We have all wondered what it could be but none of us can come up with anything. That brings me to the interview. The people we want to speak to are the residents of the home he was at. I'm interested in knowing if any of you recognize the person we're getting ready to question and if you think it's someone Officer McClain may have known. Also we want to make sure without a shadow of a doubt that this person wasn't at all tied to the murder, so your help is very important. We're hoping that the interview with them will reveal more information. We wanted you all to be here during the interview because once we talk to them we're certain that we won't be able to keep information about them or the tape confidential for much longer. That's why we wanted to have the interview and have you all listen to the tape all at one time."

"I understand," Simone said.

CHAPTER 21

Simone

Sergeant Tooley continued, "Okay. Well, if everyone is ready we'll go ahead with the interview." The ladies nodded. "The interviews will be conducted by Detective Carson who you see on the other side of this window. We can see into that room but they won't see us."

"Okay." Big Momma spoke for all of them.

Sergeant Tooley went over to the wall to the left of the large window and pushed a red button. He spoke into a speaker. "Detective Carson, please bring the first woman in." The gentleman behind the glass window got up from his chair and walked through a door next to the table he was sitting at.

A woman appearing to be in her late thirties to middle forties walked into the room on the other side of the window after a few minutes.

"Does she look familiar?" Sergeant Tooley asked.

"Not at all," Simone replied. Summer and Big Momma shook their heads in agreement.

The woman looked frustrated and chewed her gum hard as if she hadn't eaten in days. "How much longer is this going to take? You've had me up in here for over an hour now. I don't have all day, and I'm sick of all this waitin'."

Detective Carson responded, "Ma'am, I'm sorry for your wait. As I told you earlier, we've been very busy but hopefully we'll be done soon."

Without waiting for an offer to sit down, the woman flopped down in a wooden chair and let out a long, deep breath of frustration.

Detective Carson went to the other chair and sat down.

"Now ma'am, as I told you, we want to ask you some questions about what happened the day your house was burglarized and everything that happened during your visit with the officer that came to take your report."

"What do you mean, everything that happened? Someone broke in my house, I called the police, you sent somebody out, and y'all did nothin' to get my stuff back. That's what happened. What else do you wanna know?" She turned her head, studied her fingernails, and went back to chewing the gum, popping it loudly as she chewed.

Detective Carson replied, "Ma'am, the more cooperative you are with us, the easier and quicker this will be for everyone."

"Easier for everyone? Easier for who? Not me! I got my stuff stolen, y'all took y'all time comin' like y'all always do because you couldn't care less about us in the projects. If I was up north you woulda been there in a matter of minutes. Talkin' about easier for everyone. Hmmph." The woman rolled her eyes and let out another deep breath and went back to cracking her gum.

Detective Carson continued. "Ma'am, I'm sorry about what

happened to you, but right now I need to know everything that happened from the time Officer McClain got to your house until he left."

The woman had a blank look on her face and it was obvious that she had no intentions of cooperating.

Frustrated, Detective Carson stood up and placed both of his hands on the table with his palms down facing the woman.

She looked up at him with a frown on her face. "Who do you think you are, lookin' at me like that?"

He didn't move but spoke in a much more stern and demanding voice. "Ma'am, let me make this easier for you. We are investigating the murder of an officer which we take very seriously. This happened right outside of your home and we have evidence that something happened inside your home during that visit that could link you to this case. Now, we can get the information we need from you either voluntarily or we can get it involuntarily. It's up to you. If you choose to continue being difficult, it'll only take me a couple of hours to get the warrants I need to arrest you, and trust me, that will be much more inconvenient for you and will definitely take a whole lot more of your time than the process we are going through right now. Now, I'll ask you again, please tell me everything that happened after Officer McClain arrived at your home on the day that you reported that there was a burglary at your home."

The woman began shifting in her chair. She was no longer popping the gum and her appearance changed from frustrated to shocked at Detective Carson's sudden change in personality. She seemed nervous, and Detective Carson took notice of her change.

She began speaking. "What? What do you mean you have

evidence that could link me to that policeman's murder? I had nothing to do with that."

"Ma'am, at this time we're not at all saying that you had anything to do with it. We only want to ask you some questions. However, we need your full cooperation or we will have to take a different course of action. We know something happened in your home other than the officer taking a report. He was there for a very long time and we need to know why."

The officer's statement about how long David was there made Simone very curious but she continued to listen intently.

"You can begin, and please don't leave anything out." Detective Carson pushed a tape recorder towards her. "Please speak loudly into the recorder and state your name for the record."

The woman continued shifting in her chair and looked more nervous than before. She began speaking. This time more calmly. "My name is Donna Johnson. The officer came to my apartment and I gave him a report of all the things that were missin'."

Detective Carson stood up against the wall and stuck his hands in his pockets. "Okay, let me ask you this. I need an honest answer. If we find out you've been dishonest with us we will have to book you and your entire position with us will change." He stopped and studied her reaction. She looked worried and crossed her arms. She put one arm on top and then switched their positions as if she didn't know what to do with them. She was looking at the wall to the side of her.

He continued speaking in a very stern voice. This time he enunciated every word. "Officer McClain is the officer that came to your home. Did you know him personally?"

Her eyes got wide and she began rubbing her hands together. She didn't respond right away.

Detective Carson leaned in towards her on the table again and said, "Ma'am?"

"Yeah?"

Detective Carson leaned in closer to her face and asked, "Did you know him?"

She responded, "He was someone I knew years ago. We had a lot of the same friends."

Simone was confused. *I knew all of David's friends, male and female. What is this lady talking about? I've never seen her. What friends did they have in common?* She continued listening.

Detective Carson now leaned back on the wall with his arms folded again. He asked, "What happened when he came to your apartment?"

She was looking down at her lap. Then, as if she was finally surrendering, she looked up at him and sighed.

Simone hoped that meant they were finally going to get somewhere. She was getting impatient and very irritated with the lady for going around and around the question. *What is she going to say next?*

CHAPTER 22

Donna

"Okay. What had happened was, I heard somebody knock on my door. I was still nervous and upset about the burglary. I didn't know if whoever did it would come back or not. I went to the door and asked who was there. The policeman spoke and said it was Officer McClain with the Chicago Police Department. I didn't realize at that time that I knew him. I told him to show me his badge. I looked through the peephole and saw the badge. I let him in and I couldn't believe it was David McClain. He was obviously shocked to see me too.

Her mind drifted back to that day of the burglary as she gave her account of what happened at her apartment.

"Hello. Wow! I didn't expect to see you here. I'm here about the break in."

"Well hello, David. It's been a while."

"Yes, it has. Are you okay? I'm sorry this happened."

"Yeah, me too."

"How have you been doing, Donna?" David looked over her shoulder into the apartment. He seemed genuinely concerned for her.

She looked around her apartment with great disappointment. "I've been surviving. I'm here but I'd much rather be somewhere else other than this dump, especially now that these no good thugs broke in and took all my stuff. This is the third time they done broke in here. I'm sick of this sh—" She caught herself, remembering that David wasn't a fan of profanity. "Stuff. What I'm trying to say is that I feel like they are taking over. I don't even feel comfortable in my own apartment. The living conditions around here get worse every day."

David felt bad for her. "I'm sorry to hear that. Can you tell me exactly what happened?" He pulled out a pad of paper and a pen from his pocket.

"We had been out to the grocery store. When we got home, I noticed that my door was opened. We didn't come in right away. We stood outside the door peeking in from the side trying to see if we could see or hear anyone inside. After it appeared that no one was inside, we slowly walked in and began walking all through the apartment noticing that my sh—ahhh, ahhh..." She caught herself again. "I noticed that my stuff had been stolen and my whole apartment had been ransacked. At that time we called the police and then you showed up about an hour later."

David looked around the apartment as if he was looking for someone else but clearly didn't see anyone else there besides her. She knew David had always been a thinker. Did he wonder if she was speaking of a boyfriend? Donna was known to always keep a male friend in her life. He probably guessed things hadn't changed a whole lot over the years.

"Sorry it took so long. Unfortunately, officers aren't always quick to respond right away to calls for this area because—well, as you know this is a very high crime area and there's always something going on." David shook his head in frustration. "I'm still trying to get the department to change that though." She could tell he felt bad for her and was sorry to see that her living conditions were so bad.

David's sympathy caused her anger toward the police and their lack of concern for the people in her projects to mellow temporarily. Somehow just knowing that David was on the force gave her hope for her sad and dangerous surroundings. In that moment she recognized David to be the same kind, gentle, and caring man that she'd met almost twenty years ago.

David spoke and shook her out of her thoughts. "So what all was stolen?"

"They took my TV and stereo. I had my bill money which was four hundred dollars in my dresser drawer. That's gone. They took my daughter's laptop and iPod. Do you know how long it took me to save so I could get her that stuff? They took some of her jewelry and her TV too."

David was writing fast trying to get it all down and stopped when Donna mentioned her daughter. He looked up.

"You have a daughter now, huh?" David asked.

"Yes, believe it or not, I do. I know. I was the last person everyone would have expected to have a child but I did," Donna responded.

"Wow, that's great. I'm happy for you. A child is truly one of the best blessings God can give a person. I know that my daughter is the best thing that happened to me."

Donna nodded.

"Well, I've got your report. You should hear from the detective in a few days. In the meantime, be careful around here and don't hesitate to call us if something else happens." *He began walking toward the door.*

Donna looked at him for a moment as if she was trying to remember something.

"One more thing before you go. Can you hold on a quick second?" *Without waiting for a response she turned and walked away into another room. When she returned she came back with a teenage girl. David looked at her. He was speechless.*

"David, I'd like you to meet my daughter." *She paused.* "I'd like you to meet our daughter."

CHAPTER 23

Simone

SIMONE WAS IN shock and steaming mad. Coming to her feet, she yelled, "That tramp is lying. David would never keep something like that from me." She wanted to put her hands around that woman's neck. Hearing David's name come out of that woman's mouth made her skin crawl. She said it so comfortably. It just made Simone feel sick to her stomach. Big Momma grabbed her hand.

"Shhhh. Calm down, baby. Let's hear her out. I don't like what I'm hearing either but we need to see where this is going."

Simone took a deep breath and sat back down. It didn't keep her mind from racing. She thought, *Oh my God! This evil woman is trying to destroy David's name. Who is she?* Then she remembered something. *She said her daughter was a teenager. Could she be the woman David told me he was in a relationship with not long before he met me? Could this be her trying to come now with this lie, claiming that her daughter belongs to David so that she can get some money from his death?* Her mind continued to race.

"I know she has to be lying. David would never keep something like that from me. He said that he dated a woman only for a short time and it didn't work out because the woman didn't want anything out of life. But, her?" Simone turned up her nose and pointed to the woman. She continued talking fast.

"David would have to have been delirious. There's no way he could have a child with this trifling sleaze bag. I'm certain. She's an opportunist, running a scam. She wants money. Why else would she bring up something like that all these years later and at a time like this if it weren't for money? If she did date David, which I highly doubt, but if she did, could she still be upset that their relationship didn't work out and trying to take her revenge now by making this lie up about her child being his?"

"She very well could be," Sergeant Tooley agreed.

"Well, you know what? David isn't here to defend himself and I will not let this lowlife woman drag my late husband's name through the mud. The detective needs to ask her some more questions. She hasn't told him anything that would make me believe that her child belongs to David. How did they meet? Who are these friends she claims used to hang out with her and David?"

"I agree with you. Trust me, Detective Carson is good. You can count on him to ask all of the right questions that will get the answers you need," Sergeant Tooley said.

CHAPTER 24

Donna

"Okay. Now I've told you what I know. Are we done yet? I've been here a long time and my daughter is still down the hall waitin' on me. Can I leave now?" Donna asked.

Detective Carson had his head down, reviewing his notes from their interview. He raised one finger and said, "One moment." He paused. Still looking down, he continued, "Actually we're not done just yet. I still have a few more questions."

Dropping her arms beside her in defeat, Donna let out a long sigh.

Detective Carson continued looking at the papers in front of him as if he wasn't fazed by her at all. After a few minutes, he looked up and asked, "So you're saying you told Officer McClain that he was the father of your daughter, right?"

Rolling her eyes in the air, she responded, "Right."

"How did you come to have a child by him and he not know about it?"

"Are you trying to say I'm lying?"

Ma'am, just answer the question. Please."

She let out another heavy sigh and with her attitude coming back once again she began, "I had some friends named Johnny, Stacey, and Kyle. They were all mutual friends of David and Michelle. Johnny and Stacey, who were dating at the time, had a card party one day and invited us all over to their apartment. That was the first time I'd ever met David and Michelle. I thought they were a couple at first but soon found out they were just friends along with everyone else in the group. We all hit it off right away and started hanging out all the time. I was glad when I found out that David wasn't dating Michelle because I thought he was very nice looking. I tried to find out more about him, slipping in questions about him to Stacey from time to time. I wanted to know if he was dating anyone seriously and where he worked. I tried to ask in a roundabout way so that she didn't know I was interested in him, but Stacey was no fool. She picked up on it right away. She teased me about liking him and it was our ongoing, inside joke. The part that was bad about it was that David didn't seem to share the same feelings as me in the beginning. I used to say he was a stuffy dude but cute all at the same time. He was so serious.

"Anyways, after askin' Stacey all of them questions and her stringin' me along just to see me sweat, she finally told me that he wasn't seeing anyone. I was glad I didn't have to worry about someone else being in my way because he was definitely my new project. It just made things easier if he was single. Although from what I could tell, he really didn't seem all that interested in dating anyone. I didn't worry about that either. I had my eyes set on him.

"David always seemed like he had a plan for what he was going to do with his life. At the time he had been out of college for a few years and was doing security work for a small agency, but everyone in our clique knew that was only temporary. Everyone except for me. Shoot! I thought he was doing well working for that security company. I didn't see what all the fuss was about and couldn't understand why he was stressing himself so much with his so called goals." She rolled her eyes.

"I used to tell Stacey that he was too serious and focused on his dreams to worry about a relationship. We'd laugh about that and Stacey would always tell me, 'Girl, there's nothing wrong with that man having dreams. Who wants to stay in the same spot their whole life? He didn't go to college for nothing.' Then she'd tell me I needed to think bigger and I'd tell her that my thinking was just fine. She'd just shake her head and laugh at me. It took a few months of us all hanging out and my showing interest in David and he finally asked me out. At first I thought he was just inviting me to another group gathering but when everybody else told me they had different plans, I was happy to see that he finally woke up and was asking me out on a date. I figured he got tired of me flirting with him so he finally gave in and thought that if he took me out it would stop me from going after him but I was wrong. David was very nice to me. Nicer than any man I had ever been with. We hung out for a while and got kind of close. Things were going just fine. Then he got all crazy on me. He started goin' to church every time they opened the doors. He said he had always gone to church as a kid and said he had been saved at a young age but he got away from God when he went to college. He would tell me that we sinned against God and that he had asked God to forgive him. I thought he lost his rabbit mind, especially when he started askin' me to go with him to church. I told him I didn't have time for no fake, Holy Roller church people. He never stopped trying to tell me about God. I let that crazy stuff go in one ear and out the other. Around that same time he started askin' me questions like, 'What do you want to do with my life?' 'What dreams do you have?' 'Where do you want to be in five years?' I got sick of all those crazy questions. Who was thinkin' about what they was gonna be doin' in five years? All I knew about was right then. For that time I was fine with workin' at the local grocery store as a cashier. It paid my bills and it allowed me to do what I wanted to do. That's all that mattered to me. I started feelin' like he thought he was better than me 'cause he wouldn't accept me for who I was. We started arguing all the time. Well, I did most of the arguing, but anyways, my answer never changed and for some reason he kept askin' me the same stupid questions like he thought he was gonna change my mind. One day he got fed up though. I guess my *desire to do nothing more*, as he always put it, was too much for him. He told me he couldn't do it anymore and he was calling it quits. I thought he was just mad and it would pass, but he really meant it. He even stopped hangin' out with the crew. He still stayed in touch with the others, but he didn't hang with us all together. I actually stopped hangin' with our group of friends shortly after he did.

"Around that same time, I started getting sick all the time. Every day I was throwin' up three or four times a day. I could barely keep any food down and I was gaining weight. I thought it was because I was upset about David leavin' me. I started to stay away from the crew myself. A few months later I found out

I was pregnant. When everyone found out I was pregnant and about to have a baby they automatically thought it might be David's. I convinced them that I'd began seeing another man shortly after David and I stopped dating and that it was that man's baby. In reality there was no one else. I didn't want to be bothered with anybody for a while after David because I cared so much about him.

"I was so mad at him for leavin' me. I was mad at him for thinking he was better than me and for trying to make me be someone I wasn't. When that lady at the clinic told me I was three months pregnant I decided right then, that I would not let him or our friends know I was pregnant. No one would have ever found out if Stacey hadn't ran into me when I was workin' at the grocery store. I decided I would take care of my baby on my grocery store salary, and I decided that David McClain would never know that we were having a baby. In a way I felt like it was a way to pay him back for hurtin' me. I knew it would hurt him if he ever found out because he was a good man. He was the type that would want to be part of his child's life. But if he didn't want to be with me, he couldn't be part of our baby's life. Ever."

CHAPTER 25

Simone

SIMONE COULDN'T TAKE it anymore. "She said her daughter was here. I want to see her," she demanded.

"Do you need a break?" Sergeant Tooley asked with concern written all over his face.

"No, I want to see her now," Simone demanded. She had a chilling look on her face as she sat there looking into the room at Donna.

"Very well." Sergeant Tooley turned off the speaker sitting in the middle of the table that gave them sound from the other room. Then he picked up the receiver to the telephone on the wall and dialed a couple of numbers. The phone rang on the other side of the wall. Detective Carson picked it up.

"Do you have any other questions for her?" He paused. They could see Detective Carson talking on the other side of the window, but could no longer hear him.

"Okay fine. Would you bring the girl in? Just ask her a few questions about what happened when Officer McClain came to their apartment."

Simone read his lips. "Will do." Detective Carson hung up the phone.

Hanging up the receiver, Sergeant Tooley walked over to the table and reached to the middle of it and turned the speaker back on. She could tell he wasn't sure what to say.

"Mrs. McClain, I feel really bad to have you all go through so much in one day. I understand your shock and anger. I have to admit, not even I was expecting to hear what she said." He paused. "I know this is very hard. I really appreciate what you all are doing."

Simone nodded. At this point all she wanted to do was see this woman's daughter and see if there was any resemblance at all to David. *What am I thinking? Of course there won't be a resemblance. This woman is lying. She's an opportunist and she think she has a chance to take advantage of our unfortunate situation. Well, that will never happen!*

Detective Carson told Donna he was bringing her daughter in for a few questions and then they would be free to leave.

"Why are you questioning her? I just told you everythang that happened." She stood from her chair.

"Ma'am, I just have a couple of questions for her." He turned and walked out the door.

"I cannot believe this!" She flopped back in her chair. She banged her fist on the table and sat back crossing her arms.

"Mom, I have to go to the restroom. I've been trying to hold it for a while and I can't anymore. I'll be right back," Summer said, opening the door.

"Okay, sweetheart."

While she waited for the detective to come back with the

girl, Simone's mind continued to run wild. She thought back to the recording she heard of David's voice saying, *"This is crazy! With all the principles I stand for and everything I've ever believed and worked for as a man, I have to wonder how something like this could happen to me."* She got chills. As much as she didn't want to admit it, David's own words make it sound like the conversation the woman said she had with David may have really happened.

Snapping out of her thoughts, Simone sat back in her chair still anxiously waiting for the detective to return with the girl. Just as she sat back the door opened. She quickly sat up looking to see what the girl would look like. Detective Carson walked through the door first and right behind him walked in a young girl around the same age as Summer. Simone gasped. She couldn't believe her eyes. Not only did the girl have a striking resemblance to David but she also looked like she could definitely be Summer's sister. *No way!* She wanted to believe that this couldn't possibly be true but the truth is there is a very close resemblance. *Lord, how could this be happening?*

Detective Carson directed the girl to sit in the chair next to her mother. He didn't waste any time beginning his line of questioning.

"Tell me about your conversation with the detective that came to your house the day your home was broken into."

Chewing gum and pushing her long red-streaked hair from her face, she began. "I was in my room and my mom came in. She told me that there was someone she wanted me to meet. I was pretty tired after a long day at school but I got up and followed her back into the living room where the policeman was standing. I was trying to figure out why she wanted me to meet the police officer. He didn't need to meet me in order to take a report for our stuff that was stolen. Then my mom told me that he was my dad. I was shocked. I didn't think I was ever going to meet him. I used to ask my mom about him all the time when I was a little girl. She would always tell me the same thing. She would say that he's not around because we didn't need him. I really didn't understand that answer since she struggled my whole life to put food on the table and to buy me clothes." She cut an evil eye at her mother and continued. "One time after we had moved, I was looking through a box for a CD I had lost and I came across an old picture of a man. On the back of the picture it had the name David written on it. I looked at the picture very closely. It wasn't a close up picture but from what I could tell I thought he resembled me a little bit. I asked my mom who he was. She hesitated but then said it was my father. She snatched the picture from me. I asked her again where he was and why I couldn't meet him. She gave me the same old answer—we didn't need him. I finally got tired of hearing the same thing so I stopped asking after that."

Detective Carson asked, "So how did Detective McClain respond when your mom introduced him to you as his daughter?"

"He looked shocked. He didn't say anything for a minute. Then I said hello to him and he said hello back." The girl continued explaining her encounter with David.

"DONNA, *how could you have kept something like this from me all these years?*" David asked, undoubtedly upset.

"David, you made it crystal clear that we wouldn't be able to be together because we were so different, so I went on with my life. I found out after we broke up that I was pregnant, but by that time I had made it up in my mind that I was movin' on. I told myself that we didn't need you."

"Donna, don't you think that was being selfish? Don't you think she deserved to know her father and that I might want to know my daughter?" Tears welled up in his eyes.

"No, I didn't think it was selfish at all. Didn't you think it was selfish for you to try to push me to be someone I wasn't and then leave me because I didn't want to be that person?" Donna looked at him with a vindictive smirk.

"Amazing. After all these years it's still all about you, huh, Donna?" David replied.

"Mom, are you serious? I can't believe you. I've spent my whole life believing that I had a father that may have not cared about me or didn't want to know me. Can't you see that he would have been part of my life if he'd known about me?"

Donna looked at her with the same smirk. The girl turned to David with tears running down her face. "I always wondered what kind of person you were and I can see that you are a really nice man. A lot of no good dudes would have denied me if they were being told something like this after not seeing a woman for almost eighteen years."

She rolled her eyes and stood with her arms crossed. David looked at her and shook his head. He turned to his newfound daughter and put his arm around her trying to console her.

"Sweetheart, I really need time to process all of this and talk to my family but I will be in touch with you. Just know that if I had known about you there is no way I would have ever not been part *of your life. Please know that."*

"Okay." *The girl nodded as the tears continued to fall down her cheeks.*

"He said goodbye, then he turned and walked out the door. That was the first and the last time I ever saw him." With tears rolling down her face, she stared at her mother with a cold, vile look. "Maybe ten minutes later we heard gunshots and you know the rest."

CHAPTER 26

Summer

As Summer walked down the corridor, she carried a bottle of water that she asked an officer for when she left the restroom. The room had gotten very stuffy and the water was just what she needed to cool off before she went back inside. The accusations that woman was making about her dad was more than she had been able to take. She was glad she had to use the bathroom. As she approached the door to the interview room she thought, *I hope this is over soon.* She reached for the door knob with her free hand and turned it. As the door slowly opened she could hear a girl's voice.

"Maybe ten minutes later we heard gunshots and you know the rest." Not wanting to interrupt anyone, Summer walked in slowly and quietly.

All of a sudden, she couldn't move. It was as if her body had become paralyzed. Summer was speechless. She began to break into a hot sweat and her head felt like it was spinning. The bottle she was holding fell to the ground and water splattered all over the floor and on her feet.

Startled, everyone in the room turned to see what the noise was. Summer still couldn't move.

Noticing her stunned, faint look, Simone stood up and walked quickly toward Summer.

"Are you okay? What's wrong?"

She stood shaking nervously. "I–I–" were the only words Summer could manage to get out of her mouth.

Summer's legs turned to jelly and she fell. Out of nowhere Sergeant Tooley jumped behind her and caught her just as she was about to hit the floor. A few minutes later she opened her eyes and wondered why everyone was standing over her. She looked at them strangely and wondered where she was and why Sergeant Tooley was holding her. Then she realized that she was still at the police station.

"I must have blacked out." She blinked her eyes and shook her head to clear her thoughts from the awful nightmare she had just had.

"Are you okay?" Simone asked her.

Sergeant Tooley walked her to the closest chair and sat her down.

"Are you okay, Summer?" Sergeant Tooley asked.

"No, I'm not okay."

Then she turned and looked through the big picture window and realized her nightmare wasn't a nightmare at all. It was reality.

This could not be happening. On the other side of the window was the most evil person she knew, Monique Johnson, and she was claiming to be her sister.

Summer appeared to be in a trance.

"Summer?" Simone called out.

"Yes, ma'am?" She was slowly coming out of the daze.

"Baby, what's wrong?"

"Mom, that's…her".

"That's who, sweetie?"

"That, girl," she pointed toward the other room, "that's the girl that's been messing with me at school."

"Are you serious?" Simone's mouth fell open.

"Summer, you know this girl? What's been going on at school?" Sergeant Tooley frowned with a very concerned look on his face.

"She's been harassing me since before school started. I've never done anything to her. This boy named Dre likes me but she likes him and she's been bothering me since I met him."

"Hmmm," Sergeant Tooley said. He stood up and walked over to the phone on the wall. He dialed a few numbers. Detective Carson picked up the phone on the other side of the window.

"Yes, sir." His voice came loudly from the speaker on the table.

"Detective. Please ask the young lady how things changed for her after that."

"Okay, sir."

Detective Carson began speaking. "So, that must have been really tough for you, finally getting to know who your father was, and then immediately knowing that you'd never get to know him. How did that make you feel?"

"I was mad." She began to cry. "I was mad at my mother for keeping him away from me all my life. Then I hated all the thugs that I had to see every time I walked outside because I knew one of them had killed him." She paused. "I hated them because as soon as I had gotten a chance to get to know him they took him from me. I was mad at his family because they had him all of these years when I didn't even get a chance to know him. I was angry at the so called *God* those holier than thou people are always talking about. If He existed then why would He let all of this happen? I was angry with the world and I didn't care about anyone because no one had cared about me."

Listening to Monique's words caused Summer to think back. *It was right after Daddy died when Jazz and I went to Di Maio's and when I went back to school that she began harassing me. I thought it was about that dude Dre. No way. She couldn't have known Daddy was my father. Could she? We always made it a point not to tell people we were related so that my life at school was normal.* Then it hit her, *Of course she knew! She figured it out after Daddy died. His name was all over the news and I'd been out of school because of his death. Everyone at school knew that I'd lost my father who was a policeman. She put the last names together.* Although Summer knew Monique liked Dre, it still never really made sense to her why she would hate her so bad over a dude that Summer showed no interest in; especially when everyone else at school was showing Summer sympathy for her loss. It was then that Monique started to hate her and making her life miserable. Now it all made sense. Summer sat in disbelief. She had a vendetta against her all along even before Dre came into the picture. Monique Johnson was her sister.

CHAPTER 27

Summer

SUMMER HAD NO idea where she was going, but she knew she had to leave the police station immediately. After convincing her mother that she really had to go to the bathroom again and she could go alone, Summer slipped through the crowd of uptight people in the lobby and out the door of the police station. She had to process everything that had just happened and she couldn't do it in the same space that Monique Johnson was in. That girl was destroying her life in every way imaginable. She had no idea where she was going.

As Summer walked aimlessly down the streets of Chicago, her head felt like it was exploding from the series of events over the past several months that were playing over and over in her head. Even worse, her heart ached terribly. She kept pinching herself because she couldn't believe that any of what was happening could be true. She would do anything to wake up from the madness. No matter how many times she pinched herself she realized that the nightmare she was having was real.

Where can I go? There was only one place she could think of at the moment that she might find the slightest bit of peace. What she really wanted was some answers. She needed to be near her daddy to help her make sense of it all. But how could he when he was gone? She decided to go to the cemetery anyway. *Dang. I don't have my car. The cemetery is far from here. Too far to walk. Forget it. I'll walk anyway. I'll get there eventually.* She knew that's where she needed to be at that moment. Ever since her father died, going to the cemetery always gave her a sense of peace when she was thinking about him. She wanted to be as close to him as she could at that moment.

SUMMER walked through the cemetery gates. Numb and unaware that tears were running down her cheeks, she thought about how completely empty she felt. Was this someone else's life she'd been living? Who was this Summer McClain whose life was once picture perfect and was now anything but? She began going through the laundry list of things that had gone wrong in her life lately beginning with losing her father. She felt like her own life had ended after losing him, but surprisingly life went on. *Why does everything continue to spiral out of control, God?*

She thought about Antoine disappearing. She was still worried deeply about him. She knew deep down something had to be wrong because it wasn't like him. He was dependable and he was a huge part of her life. He would never just disappear unless something was wrong. *Is he dead or alive?*

Oh, God, I can't stand to lose anyone else. Please let Antoine be okay, Lord. Please protect him.

Then she thought about Jasmine. Was she losing another best friend to an eating disorder? *God, please let Jasmine get better.* Summer hadn't talked to her in over a week. Vivian found someone to provide her with onsite counseling. She really hoped Jasmine would get better. Soon.

Her phone rang. She looked at the screen. It was her mother. She sent it to voicemail and dropped her phone in her jacket pocket. She wasn't ready to talk to anyone yet.

She continued talking to God, this time aloud.

"Why am I trusting You to answer any more of my prayers? I asked You not to let Daddy die but You took him anyway. You've let my life turn into a complete mess. Nothing has gotten better. They have only gotten worse by the day. Mom and Daddy always said, 'Summer, God will never leave you or forsake you.' But you have, God. Why? Why me?"

Summer continued walking across the thick green lawn. As she walked, through her tears she studied the names on the tombstones and the dates under each name. Each of the names represented that of so many faceless people who had died over the years. Many died due to illness or an accident. Others died because of old age. But how many of the faceless people died like her father did where their lives were ripped away senselessly at the hands of violence? How many of them were innocent people who were snatched away from their family and friends without any warning? How many of those people have families that would hurt for the rest of their lives from the emptiness that was left with them? She felt helpless?

The wind was beginning to blow hard. The trees were

swaying. Summer closed her jacket over her chest. She was glad she'd brought it. She looked at the sky. The clouds were dark. She could smell the dampness in the air. A storm was definitely coming. She didn't care. She had to talk to her daddy. She continued walking and looking around for his name.

Her phone rang in her pocket. She ignored it. She reached down and picked up a twig. She broke it piece by piece as she walked and let each one drop to the ground. She felt her life had become just like that twig, broken into tiny little pieces. She felt like she could keep walking and never stop.

"God, if You're there, just please help me to get through this. Let talking to Daddy make me feel like everything is going to be okay, like I always did when he was living. Why is all of this happening? What did I do to deserve this, God?"

She felt a couple of raindrops fall on her forehead. She looked up. The sky was getting cloudy, gray, and foggy. She couldn't turn around now. Summer looked straight ahead. There it was. She'd made it to her dad's gravesite. She walked over to it and looked at the inscription on the cream and burgundy marble tombstone as if it were the first time she'd ever seen it. She read it.

Officer David C. McClain

Husband, Father, Son, Friend to all he met but most of all, a man of God's own heart.

"Just like David in the Bible." Summer smiled. Tears fell down her cheek.

She sat down on the grass next to the tombstone and rubbed her hand across his name. *If only I could hold his hand again.*

Her attention was diverted to the bouquet of flowers that were lying right below the inscription. They were beautiful. She wished her visit had been planned so she could have brought something to honor her dad. *Has mom been here? Did she leave these flowers?* she wondered. Her mom hadn't mentioned recently that she was going there. On second thought, Summer realized that she hadn't made it very easy lately to talk to since she'd been spending most of her time in her room. Maybe her mom wanted time alone with him too.

"Daddy, so much has happened since you've been gone. I wish you were here. I don't know what to do." The raindrops were coming down harder as they mixed with Summer's tears. The fog became thicker. A loud roll of thunder roared followed by a flash of lightning. Summer looked at the sky and gathered her jacket tighter across her chest.

"I know Mom and Big Momma are here for me, but I still feel so lonely. It's not the same without you. My friends are having problems. I think something bad has happened to Antoine. Jasmine has an eating disorder. It's just been crazy, Daddy. On top of everything, this girl has made my life miserable. And now she's saying she's your daughter." Summer cried uncontrollably.

"What should I do? I can't take this anymore." Summer's phone was ringing again but she continued to ignore it. The storm was getting pretty bad and it was getting darker outside, making it hard for her to see.

She knew by now her mom had to be worried about her. She figured she'd stay another ten minutes.

"Daddy, I never knew it would be like this. I—"

Summer was interrupted by the crunching sound of leaves behind her. Fear took over her body. *Was it a snake or a deer?*

She was terrified of snakes. She knew a deer would take her out. It probably wasn't a good idea to run or make a sudden move. She turned her head around slowly. She could see the image of a person standing in front of her. She could barely see their face because of the fog.

"Well, look at the little rich girl." Standing before her in the thick fog was Monique. In spite of the cold rain pouring on her, Summer's body became hot and stiff.

"Where is your tough friend Jazz now. Some friend she is. She's not here when you need her. She can't save you this time." Monique walked up to Summer and flicked her long, wet hair with her hand then pushed Summer's forehead back. She began laughing aloud and circling around the gravesite like she had a right to be there.

Summer felt more disrespected than ever before. The fear that had taken over her body moments earlier was suddenly replaced with anger. Before she knew it she'd jumped from the ground and lunged toward Monique. They fell to the ground. Summer was on top of her. The rain continued to pour down. The lightning lit up the sky. Summer pounded Monique's face over and over and over again. Every single thing Monique had ever done to her flashed before her eyes. She could see herself sitting at Di Maio's with cold, sticky lemonade all over her lap. Then all the times Monique bumped into her in the hallway at school ran through her mind. She could hear every threat Monique had ever made and every mean word she'd ever said toward her was ringing in her ears. She saw every color Monique spray painted on her car flashing in her mind. *Now this heifer thinks she's going to be part of my family.*

"Never," Summer yelled. She sat with her legs straddled

across Monique as she pounded her fist harder on every inch of her face.

Monique struggled to get Summer off her, but she was too strong.

Summer's phone rang over and over. She ignored it. She kept pounding and pounding Monique's face with her wet, bloody fist. She wouldn't stop. She couldn't stop. The rage that had been pinned up in her for months wouldn't let her. She had to let it out.

"I—Hate—You! You will never, ever, be my sister. Stay away from me and stay away from my family."

The next thing Summer knew she could feel the force of someone pulling her off Monique. She had no idea who it was. She kicked out of control trying to escape their tight grip. Her foot kicked Monique's chin. Summer's arms were swinging and her legs were still flying out of control.

"Let me go!"

"Get out of here," a male voice yelled.

Monique used her hands to push her weak body up from the ground. Her face was drenched in blood mixed with rain. Her black with red tinged hair was stringy, like a mop. She stumbled backwards looking at Summer with a look of extreme shock.

"Get out of here," a male voice yelled again. Monique ran away in the dark, foggy night.

The hands holding Summer sat her down gently in the same spot she'd sat earlier next to her father's gravesite. Summer's eyes were burning from the tears and rain. She wiped her eyes with the sleeve of her jacket. She turned around to look at the man behind her but no one was there. All that was there was the thick fog dancing in the air.

Now this is creepy. She looked around her on every side, but still, she didn't see anyone.

'Summer, violence isn't the way to solve anything. God is your protector. He will never leave you or forsake you.' She heard her father's gentle voice say. She jumped to her feet and looked around. No one was there.

"Daddy?" There was no response. The only sound was that of her own heavy breathing. She looked around again hoping she would see the mystery man, but no one was there. Hoping her daddy would speak to her again she called out to him once more.

"Daddy?" Still, nothing. The wind slowed but there was a slight breeze that blew through the trees. The rain stopped, the fog began to fade and the sky became clear.

CHAPTER 28

Simone

SIMONE WAS A nervous wreck. They had waited and waited for Summer to come back from the restroom. After twenty minutes she began to worry about her. She couldn't take it anymore. She went looking for her. She didn't see anyone in the ladies room except a short, round woman standing in a mirror looking at her reflection as she teased her thin bleach blonde hair. The doors to each of the stalls swung open. No one else was in there.

She frantically rushed to the hallway where she met Sergeant Tooley.

"Summer went to the restroom but she isn't in there. It's been thirty minutes. I'm worried about her."

"Stay right here." He left and returned five minutes later.

"I've checked every inch of the station. I don't see her anywhere. Hold on a few minutes. I have an idea." After he was unable to find her anywhere, he decided to look at the tape from the camera inside the station. He saw Summer slip out the door thirty minutes earlier. He immediately sent a few cars out in search of her.

Without a second thought, Simone called Jay. She quickly briefed him on Summer leaving the police station, and told him she'd give him all the details when he got there. He drove up to the police station within ten minutes to pick her and Big Momma up and they began their own search for Summer.

"Jay, thanks for coming. I'm so worried about her. Where could she be?"

"Don't worry, Simone," he said, reaching over to hold her hand. "I promise you we'll find her."

"Jay, what is happening to our lives? We're falling apart," Simone said, fighting back tears as Jay drove down the streets of Chicago.

Big Momma sat quietly, praying in the back seat.

"Simone, I'm so sorry. I wish there was more I could say. What happened back there?"

"Well, first they had us listen to a recording David left for you on the day he was shot. He was very upset. Then they began questioning the woman who David visited right before he left the message. You know, the one woman whose house was burglarized?"

"Yeah?"

"She was claiming that David was the father of her daughter. Then they interviewed her daughter. Well, Summer ended up knowing the girl. It turns out she's the same girl that has been bullying Summer at school. When Summer saw the girl and figured out what she was claiming, you know, that she is David's daughter, Summer fainted."

"Wait a minute. Let me get this right. The woman's daughter knows Summer and has been bullying her?" Jay was shocked.

"Yes, she goes to the same school. That explains why Summer had become even more withdrawn than she already was after David's death. Anyway, when she got herself together she said she needed to use the restroom. My instincts told me to go with her, but she insisted she'd be okay by herself. I knew I should have gone with her."

"Don't blame yourself. She's definitely doing things lately that are not like her. You had no way of knowing she'd leave that police station."

"And that woman and her daughter are trying to destroy David's name and our family by telling their lies."

Jay didn't comment. For a few minutes the car was silent.

"Simone, it's true."

She looked at him with raised eyebrows. She was confused.

"When I got the message on my phone the day David was shot, I insisted that I interview the woman. They demanded that I stay away from there so I wouldn't jeopardize the investigation. My phone was confiscated and the message was taken as evidence. While they were doing their investigation, I was determined to do my own. Against their instructions I went to talk to the woman any way. She talked to me through a little space in the door with the chain on it and wouldn't tell me anything. I was so mad at that woman, Simone, I could have choked her. She would not cooperate. I can still hear her annoying voice yelling, 'You got a warrant?' When I said, no, she slammed the door in my face."

Big Momma wrapped her hands around her arms and rocked side to side, shaking her head.

"I knew from David's message something happened there but it was obvious I wasn't going to get any answers from that woman. On top of that, I felt awful because I should have been there with David to help him that day. I was frustrated because I wanted answers and I couldn't get them. I went home that evening, but the next day I stopped by the hospital to see David. You all must have stepped out to get a bite to eat or something because no one was there. I stood by his bedside talking to him. Although he couldn't answer, I felt like he could hear me. I looked up and his eyes were opening. I started to call the doctor but he told me not to leave. I apologized for not being there to help him and he told me it wasn't my fault. I asked him about that woman and what happened when he was there. Although his voice was low and groggy, I could still hear the conviction and pain that he had in his weak voice. I still hear it in my head today. He told me she was someone he dated for a very short time before he met you. Then he told me about his daughter."

"Jay, man, I looked at her and noticed right away that even underneath the bright red streaks in her hair and the heavy make-up she was wearing that she was a beautiful young girl. Although she didn't look like Donna, she did remind me of her from years ago but beyond that I knew she looked strikingly like someone else I knew. Then it hit me. She looked like my baby, Summer. Donna told me that she was my daughter and she'd kept her from me all these years because I didn't want to be with her. Jay, I was immediately overtaken by guilt. I can't believe I have a child whose entire

childhood I've missed. All because I was part of a sinful relationship with a woman that I would have never had a long-term relationship with. God saw it fit that we have a daughter together in spite of our sins. But because she knew I didn't want to be with her, she was too selfish to let me be part of our daughter's life."

"David, man, that's not your fault. You know you would have been a great father to her if you'd known about her."

"Jay, listen. If I don't make it, when the time is right I want you to tell Simone about this. She'll know the right way to tell Summer. And please, let her know that I didn't know about this and I'm sorry. Tell Simone to do right by her for me. I know my sweet Simone. She will."

"Man, don't talk like that. You're going to make it."

"Right then he closed his eyes. I panicked. I didn't know if he was dying or what. I ran and grabbed a nurse. When she came in and checked him she said his vital signs were all the same as they had been. She looked at me like I was crazy and said he was still in a coma. I think she thought something was wrong with me and I really hadn't talked to him."

Simone sat, stunned. "So she was telling the truth?" Simone couldn't believe it.

"She was. I was waiting for the right time to tell you. With the pain of losing David, it just hadn't seemed like the right time had come," Jay said.

"I always told David to get to know the women he dated and if she wasn't marriage material to move on as fast as possible. Humph. What kind of woman keeps a father from his child?" Big Momma said from the backseat.

"Big Momma, you'd be surprised. I see all kinds of things out here," Jay responded.

As much as Simone hated to admit it, she knew Jay was right because the people whose houses he went to were some of the same kids she saw in the classroom.

"It's sad, but it's true. So many parents put themselves before their children's care and well-being," Simone agreed, and then changed the subject. "Where could Summer be? She hasn't answered any of my calls. We have to find her. I'm afraid to think what more could go wrong."

CHAPTER 29

Jasmine

Jasmine took her headphones off her ears and threw them on the bed next to her with the music still playing loudly through them. Raising her head from her pillow and sitting up on the side of her bed, she picked up the phone for the tenth time to call Summer.

Where is she? It wasn't like Summer not to answer her calls. She wanted to let her know that she was back from counseling and doing good. She knew Summer was pretty worried about her when she left. Now she was worried about Summer. *Maybe I should try calling her house again.* Every time she called there she got the voicemail. Usually Big Momma would answer the phone if no one else answered. Jasmine called the house again anyway. Still no answer. This time she just hung up. She figured there was no use in leaving another message. Sitting on the edge of her bed, she took a deep breath. "Let me try her cell phone one more time."

"Summer!" she yelled, surprised that she had actually answered the phone that time. "I've called you a thousand times. I was worried about you. Why haven't you been answering the phone?"

"It's a long story, Jazz."

Not accepting Summer's lame excuse, Jasmine responded, "What do you mean it's a long story? I've got time."

"I can't talk right now. I thought you were still gone."

"No. I'm back. That's why I was calling you. Now tell me what's going on?" Summer sounded terrible and Jasmine could tell she was trying to change the subject. "Come and get me. We can get something to eat," Jasmine continued.

"I don't have my car with me and it was vandalized anyway."

"What?"

"Yeah, another long story. I'll tell you about everything when I see you," Summer said flatly.

"Where are you, and what are you doing right now?"

"I'm on the bus and I'm almost downtown."

"On a bus? You?" Jasmine paused as if she was waiting for Summer to respond. "Never mind. I'll catch a bus and meet you downtown. Meet me at Grant Park." Jasmine's voice indicated that she was not going to take no for an answer.

"Okay. I'll see you there," was all Summer said before hanging up.

CHAPTER 30

Summer

SUMMER SAT ON the bus gazing out the raindrop covered window that separated her from the rest of the world. Separated from the people who were going on with their lives while she lived in what felt like purgatory. With the palm of her hand against the window, she looked at all the people who seemed so happy. She thought about how isolated she felt and wondered what it would feel like to be on the other side again. Chills ran through her body from her wet clothes that clung to her. Her wet hair lay limp on her shoulders. She snapped out of her daydream as the bus came to a sudden halt. She realized that she was at her stop. As soon as she stepped off the bus, she was startled by Jasmine's overly excited greeting.

"Summer!" she yelled, running up to her. Summer grabbed her and embraced her in a big bear hug. As quick as she embraced her she quickly let go, stepped back and looked at Summer.

She gasped. "What happened to you? You look a mess. Your hair and clothes. Look at your hands. They're all scraped up and bloody."

Summer took a deep breath. As they walked to Grant Park, she brought Jasmine up to speed on everything that happened beginning at the police station with Sergeant Tooley telling them they were close to solving the case of her dad's murder to everything with Monique and her mother and everything that happened at the cemetery. Jasmine was speechless. She walked with her mouth open in disbelief.

She finally spoke, "Are you kidding me? Monique Johnson is your sister?"

Summer hated hearing Monique's name and the word "sister" in the same breath.

"That's what she and her mother are claiming. When I think back to when she started harassing me, it was right after my daddy died. I think they may be telling the truth."

"I hate to say this, Summer, because I can't stand her even more now, but when I think about it, she does kinda look like you."

Summer cringed. "Jazz, *don't* say that." The thought of Monique being her sister was bad enough but she didn't want to be reminded of the fact that they did favor each other.

"Remember we used to get so mad at Antoine when he used to say you two looked alike? We finally got him to stop saying it because we'd get so mad at him."

"Please don't remind me. The thought of it all makes me sick to my stomach. It feels like someone punched me in it."

"I'm sorry. Anyway, girl, did you kill her?" Jasmine chuckled, reaching for Summer's hands. "You must have because your hands look like you've been pounding on rocks. Ooohhh, that's what she get. I just wish I would have gotten to her first."

Jasmine mentioning her scarred up, bloody hands reminded Summer of how badly they were throbbing. Somewhat embarrassed, she gently stuffed her hands in her jacket pockets. Fighting Monique the way she did was against everything she'd ever been taught.

Wanting to ignore Jasmine's last question, Summer walked ahead of her stepping onto the grass of the park. She knew Jasmine wouldn't stop talking, so she responded, "I don't want to talk about her anymore. Let's see if we can find somewhere to sit."

"I can't believe it's so many people out here after all that rain we had earlier," Jasmine said.

Summer looked around. There were quite a few people hanging out. There were a couple of guys standing around talking and a lady who was deep into a conversation on her cell phone. Summer figured she must have been arguing with a boyfriend. From the frown on her face and the way she was pointing her finger as if he was standing in front of her, she was reading him his rights and wasn't about to lose that argument. Across the lawn on the other side of the park there was a guy on a bench reading a book and several other people just standing around doing nothing at all.

"Let's sit here," Jasmine said, walking up to an unoccupied bench.

Wanting to ensure that the conversation stayed diverted from Monique and all that had happened with her and her father's case, Summer decided she'd ask Jasmine about how she was doing with her bulimia and about counseling. Jasmine gave her a detailed account of how the counselors worked with her. She said that she was put on an antidepressant drug that she would have to take for a while along with being on a regular diet of three meals a day.

"How did you become bulimic?" Summer asked.

"Most people become bulimic because they are in some way unhappy with their body."

"You were unhappy with your body? You're the perfect size. Not as skinny as me, but not even close to being fat. I don't get it."

"It's hard to explain. People who suffer from bulimia look in the mirror and what they see is not what others see when they look at them. Everyone else see normal, we see fat. Then it causes us to want to diet and that usually leads to other bad habits such as binge eating, taking laxatives, or causing ourselves to vomit. The counselors said I was fortunate I got help when I did because too much longer would have caused damage to my body."

"Wow. You were going through a whole lot. I had no idea. I really didn't know anything about bulimia."

"Yeah, a lot of people don't. Like me, a lot of people going through it don't even know what's going on with them. They're just trying to be happy with what they see in the mirror. I wasn't so happy with your mom at first for telling my mom and making me go to counseling, but now, I'm really glad she did. I feel so much better than I did when I was going through that. I had no idea of the danger I was putting my health in. You should have seen some of the pictures they showed us of people that had it really bad. Some of their teeth were rotted. Sometimes people get swollen cheeks and broken blood vessels in the eyes. Thank God none of that happened to me. Could you see me walking around looking like that?" Jasmine frowned.

"No, I couldn't."

"I'm even back to normal with my diet and eating habits. A lot of people still have trouble even after counseling," Jasmine said with a smile. Summer could tell she really was thankful.

"Well, I'm glad you're okay. I was really worried about you. I just wish you had told me what was going on."

"I know. I'm sorry I didn't talk to you. It was embarrassing. There were a few times I tried to tell you, but I couldn't figure out how. I thought you would think I was some kind of freak or something. I should have known I could have talked to you though."

"Yeah, you could have." Summer tried to hide her disappointment.

Startled by her phone ringing, Summer took it out of her pocket to look at the screen, but changed her mind and stuck it back into her pocket without looking. She knew it had to be her mother. She was afraid to answer it.

"Why didn't you answer your phone?" Jasmine questioned. Summer gave her a guilty look.

"You still haven't talked to your mom? She doesn't know you're okay?" Jasmine squealed.

"Don't make me feel worse than I already do, Jazz."

"I'm not trying to make you feel bad, but you know you're wrong for making your mother worry about you like that."

"Okay, okay," Summer said, looking across the park's lawn and away from Jasmine. She felt bad enough and was tired of Jasmine pressuring her.

"Oh my gosh! Oh—My—Gosh!" Summer yelled and jumped to her feet.

"What's wrong?" Jasmine asked, jumping to her feet as well.

Without responding, Summer ran across the park. Jasmine ran behind her.

"Where are you going?" Jasmine yelled with no response from Summer. "Slow down. Why do you always do this to me?" Jasmine yelled, trying to catch Summer who ran much faster than she did. "You're scaring me!"

The sounds around Summer were all muffled. She had blocked out everything that was going on around her and her mind raced. It was going faster than her feet, if that was possible. *No way. It can't be.* She came to a sudden stop. She was stunned. She tried to speak but nothing came out. She looked around. The people around her must have thought she was crazy.

The men who were talking earlier looked at her strangely. Even the lady who had been arguing on her phone paused from her conversation to look up at her. The guy on the bench in front of her, who was looking around just a minute before, was now obviously engrossed in the book he was reading. His lowered head was covered by the hood of a gray hoodie. He rested his elbow on a blue backpack sitting next to him on the bench.

Summer looked around at each person as they observed her awkward behavior. She didn't have time to worry about what they thought. She had to find a way to push the words she desperately wanted to say from her mouth.

"H–hey," Summer said to the hooded guy.

Looking up from his book he responded, "Hey."

"It is you." Tears welled up in Summer's eyes. "Antoine. Where have you been?"

"Hey, Summer. It's really complicated. I can't go into it right now."

Jasmine ran up behind Summer, holding her chest and bent over. She was completely out of breath. She looked up. "Antoine?" She barely got out the words.

"What do you mean you can't go into it right now? You disappear for months during a time that I could have used a friend the most, and you come back and all you can say is 'It's complicated' with no explanation?"

Antoine didn't respond. He looked around nervously.

"Aww, it's like that? What's wrong with you? You call yourself my friend, one of my best friends, and you do this to me?" Summer continued to rant.

Antoine looked around again on each side of him and then said, "Look Summer. I can't talk right now. I need you to leave."

Summer chuckled. She couldn't believe what she was hearing. "You need me to leave?"

"Summer, why is it so hard for you to just listen? I said I don't want to talk to you. Leave me alone. Now do you get it? I don't want to be bothered with you."

Summer's heart sank. The tears that had welled up earlier were now running down her cheeks. *Who is this person in front of me because it is not my best friend Antoine? What is his problem?* She looked at him wondering what was really going on, and then decided she should turn around and leave. Before she could turn around she heard a voice from behind say, "Dude," Followed by an obnoxious laugh. "You really are back from the dead." Summer knew that voice anywhere and she was not in the mood. She was not up to dealing with Dre, especially after the way Antoine had just treated her and everything else that had gone wrong that day. *Why does this guy always pop up at the most inconvenient times?* Summer thought as she turned around to look at Dre.

"Awww! It's your little shawty. So you found your boy after all?"

"Man, wassup?" Antoine asked as he stood up and walked in

front of Summer and stood between her and Dre.

"Aww, I can't stand in front of her? So, she is your girl? She told me she wasn't but I can't tell by the way you're blocking. You didn't have to lie to me, girl. You ashamed of ya boy?" Dre asked.

"Dre, I didn't lie to you." Summer wondered why she was even talking to him, let alone trying to explain herself. "Whatever." She held up her hand toward Dre, dismissing him totally. She was completely frustrated with his ignorance and her feelings were still crushed by Antoine.

"Yeah, whatever. I'll catch up with you later, Shawty. I got business to take care of with your boy right now though," Dre said.

Summer turned up her nose and rolled her eyes at him. *What business does Antoine have with Dre? I've never known them to be friends.* She looked at Antoine hoping to get an answer about their odd acquaintance. Something wasn't right about the way he was acting. Deep down inside she was also hoping he'd say something kinder than what he'd said to her earlier, but he didn't even look at her. She walked over to Jasmine and continued to slowly walk away from Antoine and Dre. She wanted to make sure not to go so far that she couldn't hear what they were saying. She stood behind a large tree and pulled Jasmine in front of her.

"What was that all about? He's never talked to you like that before," Jasmine said.

"Shhhh. Hold on a minute. Listen," Summer said.

"So you came back to your senses and stopped playing ghost, huh? I wondered if you'd come through," Dre said.

"Man, wassup? I don't have time for all that side talk," Antoine said.

"Look, things are heating up since all that happened with that cop. The police are hangin' in the hood twenty-four seven. I don't know how long I can lay low. I'm outta here in a couple of weeks," Dre responded.

That cop? Summer thought. Her heart sank, but she kept listening.

"Cats were starting to wonder wassup with you. First, you got out the game and became all studious. Don't get me wrong. I don't have a problem with anybody going to school but after all that, you went ghost after that cop got killed. I left you all them messages and you never called back. Next thing I knew, you changed your number. Man, I'ma keep it one hundred with you. I just gotta know you can be trusted," Dre said.

"Man, I ain't trippin' over that cop. He got what he had comin'. I just had to lay low myself for a while. Things got way out of control. I didn't want to get caught up. Anyway, wassup? One of your messages said you had an offer I couldn't refuse. Well, here I am." Antoine sounded irritated.

"Look, you know I'm headed to the University of Kentucky on a basketball scholarship in two weeks. I know you headed out yourself. I thought a few stacks might make your trip a little easier and hopefully it's enough to make you forget about what happened that day," Dre continued.

"Let me see what you got," Antoine said.

Summer peeked around the tree to see what was going on. Dre reached down in his pockets and pulled out two large stacks of bills and handed them to Antoine.

"I forgot what happened already." Antoine looked around, then took the money and stuck it down in his backpack.

Dre let out a snarky laugh. "I really didn't think you would show up, but you came through. It was nice doing business with you, my man," Dre said.

Antoine looked at him and raised his chin up and down. Dre did the same and walked away.

Summer fell back against the tree. She wondered what had just happened. That was not the Antoine she knew. Or did she ever know him at all? "Let's go."

"Did you hear that? What is going on between them?" Jasmine asked.

"I don't know. I just—" Summer was interrupted by the sound of screeching tire wheels followed by loud sirens. The evening sky was suddenly lit up with red and blue lights. She looked around and it seemed like everyone standing around her was closing in on her. The men that were talking to one another earlier and the woman that was talking on the phone were all running full speed toward her. *What is going on?* As the men got closer they ran past her and pounced on top of Dre knocking him to the ground. The woman grabbed Antoine and turned him around with his arms behind his back, then handcuffed him.

Dre was fighting profusely, trying to get out of the men's grip, but it wasn't working. They were tougher and stronger than his thin frame was. The woman snatched Antoine from behind and dragged him over to where Dre and the men were.

"You are both under arrest," the taller of the two men said, "for the murder of Officer David McClain," the man continued. "You have the right to remain silent. Anything you say can and will…"

Blah is how everything sounded after that to Summer. She gasped. She felt as if someone had knocked the air out of her. She stood in disbelief watching the scene take place before her eyes. She never thought she could hate anyone more than she hated Monique. But at that moment, a hate she never knew filled her. A hatred for Antoine. He'd deceived her all along. He'd pretended to change his life when her dad helped him. Her dad brought him into their family and accepted him like he was the son he never had. And this is the payback he gets. Antoine took part in killing him. Tears flowed from Summer's eyes. She would never trust anyone again and she definitely wouldn't help anyone. Look what it got her father.

"Oh my gosh! Antoine and Dre killed your dad," Jasmine yelled. Summer stood stoic looking at Antoine and Dre being shoved into the patrol car with its lights flashing.

An officer walked over to Summer and Jasmine. "Are you girls okay?"

Summer stood speechless.

Still shocked, Jasmine responded for both of them. "Yes, we're fine."

Out of nowhere, Simone and Jay walked up.

"Summer. Are you okay?" Simone asked in a panic.

All Summer could do was shake her head.

"We were worried about you. You all shouldn't be out here," Jay chimed in.

"Do you have any idea how much you scared us? I've been calling you all day. You could have been hurt out here. What happened to you? Look at you, honey. You look a mess," Simone said.

Summer still couldn't find the words to speak.

"Everything will be okay. Come on. Let's go." Her mother wrapped her arms around her and walked her to Jay's car.

CHAPTER 31

Summer

Things around the McClain household were pretty quiet and solemn the day after Antoine and Dre were arrested. Summer finally told Simone and Big Momma about everything that happened after she walked away from the police station.

They were all in utter shock and confused about Antoine being involved in David's death. Simone called the police station a few times trying to reach Sergeant Tooley and was told each time that he was unavailable and a message would be given to him. The news reported that they'd made an arrest, but nothing else.

"They've made an arrest. I know they're busy but why hasn't he returned my calls by now?" Simone complained.

"I know it's frustrating, but I'm sure you'll hear from him," Big Momma said.

"Yeah, I guess you're right." Simone flopped down on the couch next to Summer and turned on the television. She nervously flipped through the channels stopping on Dr. Oz.

Although the TV was on, no one seemed to be really paying a lot of attention to what was being said.

There was a knock at the door. "Don't get up. I'll get it," Big Momma said, opening the door. "Hi, Jay."

"Hi, Big Momma."

"Hey, Jay. Come have a seat," Simone said, patting the spot on the couch next to her.

"Hi, Uncle Jay," Summer said as she picked at her fingernails. She was barely listening to Dr. Oz's demonstration of what clogged arteries in the heart look like when he was interrupted by a news anchor.

"We've just received word that the Chicago Police Department had a big break in the murder case of Officer David McClain, the eighteen year veteran of the Chicago police department who was gunned down in the line of duty this past June. Joy London begins our team coverage where she is live in Grant Park where two suspects were arrested yesterday. Joy."

Summer sat up straight, giving all of her attention to the newscaster. Jay stood up while Big Momma and Simone watched intently.

"Melissa, indeed this city has been rocked by the devastating murder of Officer David McClain, a true hero. After months of investigation, citizens were relieved to hear that the police arrested two suspects just yesterday, right here in Grant Park, for the murder of Officer David McClain. Police say the murder suspect, 18-year-old Andre Hughes, is a star basketball player at East High School and was headed to the University of Kentucky in the fall on a full basketball scholarship.

Yesterday we also reported about Antoine Jackson, who was arrested along with Andre Hughes for the murder. This is where this case takes an odd twist. Jackson, who has a criminal record, turned from the streets a few years ago. The victim, Officer McClain, took a personal interest in Jackson and made a commitment to help him change his life. It turns out Jackson..." Jay turned off the television.

"What are you doing? They were just going to give details about what happened with Antoine and Dre killing David. I can't get Sergeant Tooley to call me back. We need to hear this. Turn it back on," Simone said.

"You all don't need to hear it on the news. That's why I'm here. I just left Sergeant Tooley. I wanted to tell you what happened," Jay said.

"Well," Simone insisted.

"It turns out that Antoine was just as committed and loyal to David in his death as David was to him when he was alive."

"What do you mean he was committed and faithful to Daddy? He and Dre murdered my daddy." Summer was confused and irritated by Jay's claim.

"Well, not exactly. Antoine wasn't a suspect at all. He was actually working undercover for the police all along to help solve David's murder. Ironically, he just happened to be on the scene and witnessed the whole encounter that began when David approached Dre about that case with the girl who committed suicide months earlier due to bullying in the sexting case."

"You mean Megan?" Summer said.

"Yes, the girl at your school. Through David's investigation of that case, he discovered that Dre was the initiator of the picture going around. When David approached Dre, an altercation ensued, resulting in Dre shooting him. The police investigation found that Dre panicked and shot David because he feared losing his scholarship and a chance at a better life. They couldn't have gotten him without Antoine. Because of his bravery and his willingness to help the police, we along with the entire community can rest a lot easier now knowing the scum that murdered David is now behind bars. Antoine isn't a murderer at all. He's a hero."

Summer sat in disbelief. Suddenly her mind drifted back to the day at the police station. "Oh my gosh! The voices," Summer yelled, standing to her feet.

"What voices? What are you talking about, honey?" Simone asked, looking at Summer strangely.

"The voices on the recording we heard at the police station. That was Antoine. He was trying to stop Dre from shooting Daddy," Summer said, putting her hand over her mouth.

"Oh my Lord. You're right," Simone replied just as shocked.

"Antoine was helping find Daddy's murderer all along. I can't believe I doubted him. He'll never forgive me," Summer said, staring at the blank television.

"Baby, who could blame you? As well as we all know Antoine, that's how it looked. The media thought he did it. That's the way it looked to everyone. Only Antoine and the police knew what he had to do with it. He's your friend. Just talk to him. I've got a feeling everything's going to work out just fine," Simone said compassionately.

CHAPTER 32

Summer

AFTER SUMMER'S LIFE was turned upside down and filled with what felt like daily drama, she hadn't been able to imagine her life ever being drama free again. To her surprise, things had begun to mellow out for her and everyone else in the months that followed.

She and Antoine slowly mended their relationship back together. After all the months apart and everything that had happened to both of them, it seemed like they were strangers, getting to know one another all over again.

Jasmine continued to take one day at a time as she and her mother worked through her recovery from bulimia. Every day she felt stronger. After her secret was out and she got help, she was thankful that Simone recognized what was going on with her and stepped in. It was a monumental change in her life. She decided after all she went through that when she went to college the next year, she wanted to study to be a counselor to help young people through the types of issues she'd been dealing with. She told Summer that she was touched by how supportive she had been and decided she would never keep anything from her again. They made a pact that neither of them would keep secrets.

Summer still worried about her Uncle Jay. He acted like everything was okay, but Zoe kept them updated on what was really going on. She felt he had been suffering from depression. So much so that she withdrew from Art School after finally deciding to pursue her career as an artist.

"Zoe, I hope you'll decide to sign up again soon. You have a God-given talent and I promise you, you'll never feel fulfilled if you don't make the choice to chase your dream. Remember Picasso's quote?" Summer heard Simone say to Zoe on the phone. She told Simone she would but she felt she had to help Jay get through this tough time.

When the case was solved and Dre sat in jail waiting for trial, Jay was asked to come back to work but told them no. He said he couldn't imagine going back to work without David and on top of that, he said he couldn't bring himself to go back to a department that he felt betrayed him. He insisted he should have been able to help find David's murderer at the very least, since he hadn't been there for him the day he was shot.

In the meantime, with him having a lot more time on his hands, he was spending more time with Zoe. Simone gave him a hard time every chance she got about not asking Zoe for her hand in marriage yet. Jay always laughed and told her she sounded just like David.

Big Momma's spirit was picking up and she was still doing what she loved, spending most of her time in the kitchen. She was still cooking comfort food for their family that was laced with her touch of love and daily prayers. Now Summer understood why Big Momma always said that their family's strength was in the Lord. She realized now more than ever that Big Momma was their rock and that she too was getting stronger each day as she healed from the pain of losing her only son. She was able to help them see how much closer they all were not only to each other but more importantly to God. She also helped them to see that God was still working, even in times of heartache and pain.

As bad as Summer still hurt, her heart broke even more for her mom. She watched her sometimes sitting in her room looking at pictures of her dad. She knew her mom missed him more than she could ever be able to explain. He was the only man she had ever loved. Summer was amazed at how in spite of her pain, her mom was adjusting and learning to go through life without him. She remembered when her mom went back to school. She was so much more cheerful when she came home. She told them that working with her children had been surprisingly comforting. *The children heard that I lost my husband. As soon as they saw me they showered me with hugs,* she recalled her mother saying. *Now it's become an everyday ritual. It's funny. Without me telling them it was like they knew their hugs warmed my heart and made the day easier for me to get through.*

Simone told Big Momma and Summer on many occasions that knowing she had them and the strength of the Lord on her side, helped her to get stronger every day. She admitted that some days were definitely tougher than others.

Summer knew her mother was being strong for her. *"Your dad and I had plans for you to flourish and grow into a beautiful, strong, successful woman, Summer. I have to see that our plans are followed through."* Summer didn't think she could ever love her mom anymore but at that moment she had. As tough as things were for her, her top priority was still Summer.

She knew her mom still had the weight of knowing that her dad really did have another daughter that wasn't theirs together. After much prayer Simone said that God had allowed her to accept that Monique was David's daughter. Summer still struggled with accepting her. Simone explained, "As hard as it is for me to do this, I have to do what David would have wanted me to do. The insurance company sent me the money from David's life insurance policy. I've set up a fund for Monique. It will be enough for her to go to college. If she chooses not to go she'll be able to get payments from the fund once she turns twenty-one years old. She'll receive equal payments that will be distributed to her over a ten year period."

Summer started to question her mother, but decided not to. She knew that once her mom made her mind up about something and she felt that it was what God and her father wanted her to do, there was no changing her mind. Vivian thought she was crazy, but she explained to her that she knew David wouldn't have had it any other way if he were alive. She knew he would have made sure that any child of his had an opportunity to have a decent life. That was the type of man he was.

As for Monique, she graduated at the end of Summer's junior year but her legal issues were far from being over. She faced a laundry list of charges including vandalism, trespassing, assault, battery, intimidation, harassment, bullying and cyberbullying for all of the things she did to Summer.

The first time Summer had seen Monique after their cemetery fight was when they went to court. Monique was there with her mother, Donna, and her public defender. Of course, Simone and Big Momma were by Summer's side along with Vivian who was there as Summer's legal representation. Simone tried to hire another attorney, arguing that Vivian was too busy with her corporate business. Vivian insisted that she represent Summer. She was livid when they realized all of the torment Monique put Summer through and went right to working on the case. She wanted to make sure herself that Monique got all she had coming to her.

Monique's demeanor in court was mostly reserved until the judge read the charges against her. She looked up from the floor and turned her attention to the judge.

"You have all of those charges against me? What about what she did to me? Look at my face." She was referring to a cut above her eye and one on the bridge of her nose.

The judge, who looked like Judge Mablean Ephriam, slammed her gavel. "Counsel, please control your client. I will not tolerate another outburst like that in my courtroom again or your client will be held in contempt. Do you understand?"

"Yes, Your Honor," responded the skinny man dressed in a blue pin-striped suit. He looked like he'd just graduated from law school. He leaned over nervously and whispered something in Monique's ear. She dropped her shoulders and went back to looking down toward the floor.

"Young lady, look at me while you're in my courtroom. You weren't looking down at the floor when you were causing havoc in this other young lady's life, now were you?"

Monique looked up. "No," she responded defiantly.

"It's no, ma'am."

"No, ma'am." Monique looked like she wanted to choke the judge.

The judge continued looking at Monique with a stern face. "I can't believe you stood up in my court to say, *What about what she did to you?* I'll go ahead and answer your question, anyway. Because of the series of events that led up to the altercation between you and Miss McClain, this court is deciding that your case is being thrown out. I'm ruling that Miss McClain was acting in self-defense."

Monique gasped.

"Surprised? Well you think about that the next time you decide you're going to bully someone, young lady." The judge was clearly perturbed with Monique. "Now, I'll continue. The plaintiff's counsel spoke to me in my chambers earlier. This is a bit of a unique request, but I'll allow it. Please address the court on how you'd like to proceed on behalf of your client."

Vivian stood up, straightening her expensive black suit. "Thank you, Your Honor. Against my better judgment," Vivian cut her eye at Monique, "My client would like to drop all charges against the defendant."

The court room became silent. All anyone could hear was the keys on the computer as the stenographer tapped on emphatically while looking over her black-rimmed glasses.

Summer would never forget the shock on Monique's face when Vivian said she wasn't going to press charges. Summer was shocked herself when she finally agreed with her mother that it was the best thing to do. Her mother kept telling her that vengeance is the Lord's and Monique had to pay for her sins.

"I will respect the plaintiff's wishes. However, I am not going to let you off the hook completely, Miss Johnson. Bullying is a very serious offense. It's senseless and it ruins lives. I will rule that you will pay Miss McClain for the damage you did to her automobile. Also, you will have to do one hundred and eighty hours of community service. Half of it will have to deal with raising awareness of bullying. Hopefully, you'll think about it before you decide to harass someone in the future or damage their property. Do you have something else counselor?"

"Yes, Your Honor. Mrs. McClain would also like to set up a fund for the defendant."

The look on Monique's face after that news of her sentencing didn't measure up to the look on Donna's face when Vivian went on to explain that Simone was setting up a fund for Monique. She looked as if she had just hit the lottery until Vivian read the conditions. The smile on her face dropped immediately.

"College? And she can't get the cash until she turns twenty-one if she don't go to college? And she'll have to get the money in payments?" Donna yelped.

Gold diggin' heifer, Summer thought. *I told Mom. Why didn't she listen to me?*

Simone was obviously irritated by Donna's unappreciative attitude. She looked at her and rolled her eyes. The judge was evidently not happy with it either. She slammed her gavel again. "Didn't I say no more outbursts in my courtroom? Don't test me." The judge narrowed her eyes at Donna.

Vivian now directed her comments directly to Donna, "Ma'am, Mrs. McClain doesn't owe you anything. Out of the generosity of her heart, she wanted to put your daughter in a position so that she will have a promising future seeing that she is the late Mr. McClain's daughter. Those are the conditions," Vivian said with finality.

They hadn't seen Monique or her mother since then.

EPILOGUE

One year later

Neither of them could believe that it was their graduation day. Summer and Antoine sat in a park a few blocks from the school. Whenever they hung out, he often brought up the conversation he had with her that day at the park. No matter how many times she said she'd forgiven him, the guilt had never left him for how awful he had treated her.

"Summer, I want to apologize again for how I talked to you back when I was working undercover for the police. You know the only reason I did that was because the police had me wired to help get Dre's confession and I didn't want you to get hurt."

"Antoine, if you apologize to me one more time. This has to be the one thousandth time you've said you were sorry."

"I know, but I feel really bad. I hate that I hurt you. You don't know how hard it was for me to talk to you like that, but I was so worried you were going to get hurt once the cops moved in on Dre. I never expected for you and Jasmine to show up at that moment," Antoine explained.

"I know. I forgave you as soon as I knew what was going on. You were trying to protect me and if anything, I owe you. If it weren't for you, they may have never caught that punk, Dre." She fought back tears. "Thanks, Antoine. You know you're the brother I never had." She smiled and nudged him with her elbow.

She remembered how worried she was when Antoine disappeared and when she finally talked to him, worrying that their friendship was over. As usual her mother was right. Things did work out between them, and everything in all of their lives had finally calmed down. Summer couldn't have been happier when last summer was over. It had been the longest one of her life. All of their lives had been touched with individual struggles and their faith had been tested. God worked in their lives and He showed each one of them that He would get them through even the toughest of times.

Summer was so happy when Antoine came back to school after her dad's murder was solved. She was glad he was able to complete his junior year with her and Jasmine.

"About that brother stuff. You know I really like you, Summer, right?"

Summer looked confused. She couldn't believe what she thought she was hearing. Deep inside she always liked Antoine too but she never even considered that they'd be more than just buddies, close like brothers and sisters.

"You know. A lot has changed. Why don't we talk about that later." She smiled.

"Deal." Antoine returned the smile.

A lot had changed. Antoine's mother moved them to a new neighborhood. He adjusted to the change very well. He told her it felt like a new start.

"It feels weird not hearing gunshots all the time or walking outside and not having people hanging on the corners talking loud or plotting their next shady move. I don't have to feel drained every day when I walk outside because people are coming up to me trying to get me into something crazy and then having to keep telling them that's not me anymore. For the first time in my life, I kind of like being outside." He paused for a minute. "Okay. Don't laugh at what I'm getting ready to say, but the air even smells good to me now. I like hearing the sound of the birds."

Summer thought about how her dad used to tell her that they take the most simple things for granted; things that a lot of people were grateful for. She smiled.

"I won't laugh at you."

Summer thought back to the year before when she wondered if she would make it through the crazy summer of her junior year in high school. By the time the next summer rolled around she wondered what craziness it might bring. She had no idea, but she was sure that things were looking up and her dad was looking down on her from heaven. She too had begun adjusting to her new life without her dad. She was back to hanging with Jasmine and Antoine like before. In spite of not having her father in her life, she managed to have an enjoyable senior year in high school. She couldn't believe how fast the year had gone. She was surprised that every day she'd become a little bit more adjusted to her new life without her dad. There was no doubt there was still a void, but she took comfort in knowing that he was her guardian angel. She knew she had to go on because that's what he would have wanted her to do.

"So I hear you've made a decision. I think you're going to look pretty good in red and white," Summer said, smiling at Antoine.

He laughed. "Yeah, yeah. Thanks. Ol' big mouth Jazz just couldn't let me give you the good news. Yeah, since I decided to go to college, Illinois State was the best choice for me because I won't get too home sick with Jazz there with me. She'll definitely keep things live." They laughed.

"Yeah, right. She's going to keep it live alright and she's going to drive you crazy like always. I give you a week and you'll be hiding out from her."

Antoine continued, "Ahhhh, you got a point there." He laughed. "Jazz is my homey. But for real though, it's close enough that I can still be around for my moms. It gets me away from Chicago and…" He paused and gave Summer a mischievous look out of the corner of his eye with a big grin that showed all of his pearly white, straight teeth.

"And what?" Summer responded.

"And–I can start working on my career in criminal justice."

"Antoine!" she yelled, throwing her arms around him. "I'm so happy for you. Daddy would be so happy. Are you going to be a police officer?"

"I don't know. I think I will. They need more good cops like your dad and Jay. We'll have to see where I go from there." Antoine looked down at his shoes. He was silent for a moment. "Summer, I owe my whole life to Mr. M. I can't think of a better way to show how much I appreciate all he did for me. Anyway, enough about me. Have you decided what you wanna do Miss Five college offers? And which one of those big offers are you gonna take?" He smiled looking at Summer.

"You know. It bothered me a long time after Daddy died what he meant about *live with purpose. Make a difference and don't let his life be in vain.* I know what it meant, but I wanted to know exactly what *he* meant. What he wanted for me. I wanted to make him proud. Then it finally hit me. He always told me that whatever I do I should have a passion for it and he always told me that I should believe I could make a difference doing it. I'm sure now that's what he meant about living with purpose. I know if I do that I will make him proud."

"That makes sense. *Sooooo.* What did you decide?"

"Well." Summer smiled, looking at Antoine out of the corner of her eye. "After everything that happened with Daddy, I believe I have to go into law. Daddy spent his whole life trying to make a difference in the lives of people that most people don't believe in. Soooo, after all is said and done, I accepted the offer to Harvard and I'm going to be an attorney. I'm going to fight to make sure the streets are safe. Who knows, I might be a Supreme Court Justice one day."

"If anybody can, you can. That's dope." Antoine gave Summer a little shove on her arm. "We'll be like those cops and lawyers on *Law and Order* makin' things happen."

"Boy, you are so crazy. Come on." She laughed and wrapped her arm around his neck. "We have a graduation to go to."

BOOK CLUB QUESTIONS

1. Do you agree with Jay that David was wasting his time trying to help people who were committing crimes and throwing their lives away?

2. Summer told her mom that she kept the bullying to herself because she was ashamed. Could Simone have done something different to make Summer feel more comfortable with telling her what was going on? What signs did Summer show that indicated she was being bullied?

3. Social Media was one avenue that Monique used to bully Summer. How can you help to alleviate cyberbullying?

4. What things could Summer have done differently regarding the bullying instead of letting her frustration build up to the point where she finally retaliated and fought Monique?

5. What did you think about Jasmine's loyalty to Summer in standing up for her against Monique?

6. Do you think most kids are willing to stand up for their friends? If so, do you believe it would decrease the amount of bullying that takes place?

7. When Simone realized Jasmine was suffering from bulimia she immediately got involved. Do you think she was right to get involved? Do you think it's okay for parents to get in their children's friends business?

8. Is there ever a time a kid should defy their friends trust and tell their parent about a secret?

9. What did you think was going on with Antoine when he wasn't returning Summer's phone calls and ultimately moved away with no notice? Were you surprised by his loyalty in working with the police to help solve David's murder?

10. David's past sins revealed that he had a daughter out of wedlock. He had no problem taking responsibility for his actions when he found out about Monique being his daughter. As a spouse how would you have handled the situation? How do you think Simone handled it?

11. As a parent it's hard to see someone treat your child badly. Based on all that Monique did to Summer would it have been hard for you to set up an education fund for Monique and be there for her as David requested?

12. Summer's faith was first tested when David was shot and eventually died. How important was it to have had Simone and Big Momma there to support her during that tragedy? Can you think of a time where God got you through a situation and it made the next tough time better?

13. David's purpose was to be an example and help change the lives of others. He wanted Summer to make sure she knew her purpose. What do you think helped her to find her purpose? Have you found your purpose? If so, what is it? If not, what will help you determine what it is?

RESOURCES FOR THE PREVENTION OF BULLYING

❖ Stop Bullying: www.stopbullying.gov

❖ National Bullying Prevention Center: www.pacerkidsagainstbullying.org

❖ Cherlisa Starks Richardson is a motivational speaker and will attend your event to speak on the topic of bullying. For more information on all her speaking topics, visit her website at www.cherlisarichardson.com.